COWBOY RECKONING

BARB HAN

TORJAKE PUBLISHING

Editing: Ali Williams

Cover Design: Jacob's Cover Designs

To my family for unwavering love and support. I can't imagine doing life with anyone else. I love you guys with all my heart.

The sun was descending on what had been a scorching hot late summer day in Cattle Cove, Texas. Ensley Cartier had parked her car on the side of the road. She walked through the woods and entered the meadow; the beautiful oak trees a stark contrast to the memory of what had happened here.

This place. This beautiful and destructive place had taken so much from her. An icy chill ran down her spine at the memory of her younger brother walking into these woods years ago and never walking out.

Coming back to her old hometown, she'd felt compelled to stop here first. What had happened here was the reason she'd come back to town anyway.

The trail that had led to the meadow was overgrown. The same path had been well-worn years ago. A lot had changed since those innocent days in high school when her future had been bright, and she didn't have to leave the light on to sleep at night.

It was getting late and she shouldn't be out here alone. That creepy feeling she'd heard referred to as a cat walking over a grave caused her skin to goosebump.

Ensley turned tail and picked up her pace. Her hiking boot got caught on scrub brush and she nearly face-planted. She corrected her balance, grabbing hold of a tree trunk as her phone went flying and the sharp bark jabbed into her palms. She mumbled a curse.

Thankfully, her flashlight was still on and she could plainly see her phone. Getting from point A to point B was another story altogether. As she slowly stepped toward the glowing light, a noise stopped her cold.

A twig snapped behind her. Icy chills raced up her spine as she reminded herself this was deer country. Though there were probably other creatures out here that she didn't want to consider.

The hair on her arms pricked as the feeling of being watched settled over her.

Heart thundering in her chest, Ensley made a move for her cell phone, snatched it and then ducked behind a tree. She could only pray that whatever was behind her couldn't hear her out-of-control heartbeat against her ribs.

Her cell picked that moment to buzz, indicating an e-mail came through. She squeezed her hand around the speaker a few seconds too late. If there was a person behind her, there was no way he or she wouldn't have heard the noise.

Then again, the woods were alive with sounds from cicadas chirping to crickets to frogs. The wind whistled through the trees. She was grateful for the breeze in what otherwise would've been a stifling hot night.

On all fours, Ensley heard the first low and deep growl. It was the deep baritone of an animal that was close by and ready to strike. She scrambled to stand, fingers closed around her cell phone. She shone the light in the direction of the growl in time to see an incredible, massive German shepherd.

Head low to the ground, it inched toward her with raised hackles and bared teeth.

"Whoa there, buddy." Ensley remembered the years she'd spent at Cattle Cove. She'd encountered animals in the wild before. Remaining calm could mean the difference between being attacked and walking away unscathed.

Adrenaline shot through her causing her pulse to spike and a whoosh to sound in her ears. This probably wasn't the time to remember the article she'd read a long time ago about animals being able to smell fear.

Yes, she was afraid. The dog's sharp, white teeth were showing. His air snaps echoed.

Keeping her eyes constant on the animal inching toward her, carefully and purposefully, she backed up until she felt a tree. It might not be much or help for long, but maybe she could delay the dog's bite for a few critical seconds if she could manage to put the tree trunk in between them.

Not daring to take her eyes off the agitated animal, she said, "I'm not here to hurt anybody."

He barked three short barks, baring his teeth again. What was an incredible animal like this one doing out near the meadow alone? And he was impressive. Scary as all get out, too. More growling reminded her just how serious he was.

She tucked her chin to her chest, figuring the animal would go for her throat on instinct.

"Hold on there, buddy. No one's here to hurt you." She knew better than to make a quick move. Shining the flashlight from her phone onto the dog, she realized he had on a collar. That was the first bit of good news. It meant he had an owner. His carriage said he was trained.

This was the perfect time to curse the fact she had no weapon and had foolishly ran from her car into the woods, trying to ground herself in this spot without really thinking it through. She should know better. And she did.

Now, staring her mistake in the eyes, she realized the weight of her consequences.

A dog tag meant this guy had to have an owner somewhere. She knew from her limited experience with animals that German shepherds were incredibly loyal breeds. He inched closer.

Maybe she could stall long enough for his owner to show. "Who do you belong to, bud?"

Ensley bit back the irony of the thought that her life could end very near the exact same spot her teenage brother's had almost ten years ago. With questions raised about how the now-dead county coroner had handled a few cases, or more accurately *mis*handled them, she'd come back to investigate her brother's. She'd never bought the accidental death ruling or the theory her brother and his best friend had gotten into a fight that led to a murder-suicide.

She needed new evidence for the sheriff to reopen the case.

The dog moved another step toward her. His low, throaty growl a little too close for comfort. This was so not a good situation to be in. Considering the dog had tags, she might get lucky and his owner might appear. And as long as she was making wishes, she might as well go all in and pray the person wasn't out here hurt somewhere. An injured owner, or worse yet, dead, would agitate the breed of dog that had been created for protection.

Nose to the ground, the roughly seventy-to-eighty pounds of lean muscle moved toward her with military precision.

Risking a glance at the tree, she quickly assessed she wouldn't be able to climb it. Being back here brought on a tidal wave of emotions. The dog had to be picking up on all her emotions, frustrations and fears.

Since the animal was getting too close for comfort anyway, she had about one option left. It was to scream for help in the hopes the owner would hear and call off his dog.

A black snout with yellow and black markings, a pair of large, intense eyes stared her down. The longer she watched, the more she realized that the animal was flat out terrifying.

"Hold on there." Again, she used the calmest voice she could manage under the circumstances.

Making a move was pretty much now or never considering the low, throaty growls had intensified.

Ensley opened her mouth to scream just as she heard the deepest, most bone-penetrating voice calling the dog off.

"Karma."

The strong, male voice shouted out a word she didn't understand but was pretty certain was in German. She wondered whether that would make the animal some sort of police dog. Karma immediately retreated and she let out the breath she didn't realize she'd been holding.

Running into this dog reminded her of the dangers of being alone in the woods and of being back in her hometown. She could use a friend right now and especially if that person turned out to work in law enforcement. It was the only thing that made sense because she was certain an untrained dog would have attacked her.

Her thoughts instantly snapped to her brother. Cooper must have been so scared in his final few moments out here. The injustice about the case poured gasoline on the fire already burning inside her. She used that anger as fuel to be bold.

"Hello. I'm lost. Who's out there?" She trained her flashlight in the general direction where the dog had disappeared. The very real thought he could return at any moment struck. Fear rippled through her.

Ensley repeated a silent protection prayer she'd learned as a little girl. It was one she'd repeated often after her parents divorced and her mother retreated into herself as she nursed a broken heart. A few years later, she passed away.

"I said, 'hello'!" she shouted, louder this time.

A large male figure emerged, stepping out from between two trees. The growling dog was by his side. He squinted and immediately raised his hand to cover his eyes. She realized she was blinding him with her flashlight beam.

"Sorry." She lowered the light to a patch on the ground in front of her. A different kind of energy shot through her when she got a good look at the man's face. A lightning bolt struck. There was something very familiar about him.

And then, she remembered.

"Levi McGannon?" she asked, not bothering to hide her shock.

He confirmed with a nod.

Wow, that really took her back. He'd been six years ahead of her in school and the twelve-year-old girl that she'd been had a very large crush on the eldest McGannon son.

Despite Levi having five brothers and five cousins, all males, not one McGannon had been in her grade. It was impossible not to notice them, though. Everyone in town and probably all of Texas knew who they were. The McGannon family was one of the richest cattle ranching families in the state.

Declan McGannon had been a grade ahead of her and Dawson McGannon had been a grade below. But it was Levi who'd always stood out to her.

"I'm sorry. Have we met before?" Levi lowered his hands enough for her to see those penetrating dark eyes of his staring at her. He cocked his head to one side.

Ensley hadn't seen him in more than ten years. He'd gone into the military right after high school. He and his brothers were tight-knit and ran in different circles, despite her dad and stepmom doing their level best to climb the social ladder.

"No. I lived here a really long time ago. There's no reason you would remember me. We went to the same high school but not at the same time. I was there with a few of your brothers and cousins." At six-feet-four inches, he was hard to miss. Then again, all the McGannon brothers and cousins were tall and even back then had the frame for what Levi had grown into...a tall, muscled man.

His dog growled again, and Levi said another word she didn't understand.

"German?" she asked.

"Yes, he was a soldier. Bomb sniffer. He got out before his handler, who is still on active duty. Karma didn't have a place to go so a friend of mine called me up and asked if I had enough land to give him a home. Even after a year, he's...excuse me...who did you say you were again?"

"Oh, sorry. I'm Ensley Cartier."

Recognition dawned. "I know that last name."

"My father was a lawyer here. We left Cattle Cove ten years ago after my brother..." She couldn't finish that sentence. The pain was still too real, too raw.

Levi nodded his head and shot her a look of apology. "Cooper. Your brother's name."

"That's right." Hot tears burned her eyes. She ducked her head, chin-to-chest, so he wouldn't see.

"I'm really sorry. I remember hearing about that case. It was a sad situation all around." There was so much compassion in his voice, unlike what she'd heard from the families involved after the fact years ago.

His dog, however, had a laser focus on her while he stood with his hackles raised.

"I'm sorry about him." Levi motioned toward Karma. "He doesn't take to new people easily. He would probably feel better if he could make sure you don't have any sort of explosive device on you. He's very leery of anyone he doesn't know, especially if he doesn't get a chance to clear them."

"What does that mean?" She extended her arms out, shoulder height and palms down. She was careful not to make a sudden movement. "Will this help?"

"It should." Levi snapped a leash on Karma's collar and walked toward her.

The dog made quick work of sniffing her up and down. She must've passed because his aggression levels dropped and he moved beside his owner and stood.

"If you're ever with a bomb sniffing dog and he sits down, you'll want to clear out of the vicinity as fast as possible," Levi informed.

"Good to know." She had no plans to spend more time around a dog trained to sniff bombs than she had to. Her heart went out to the dog, though. From everything she'd heard, dogs and their handlers became very close. Separating them seemed cruel to her, but at least this guy seemed to have found someone who cared.

The McGannons owned acres and acres of land. A hundred? A thousand?

Her father had chomped at the bit to be their will and trust attorney, but McGannons weren't country club types and they already had a lawyer. If anything, she respected them even more for their down-to-earth qualities. If her father had been more like them, she imagined she and her brother would've had a very different upbringing. One filled with Sunday suppers around the dining table and home-cooked meals.

"Why did you name your dog Karma? Was he discharged with that name?"

"No. I gave him a different name for a different life. His original name was better off buried with his past. I renamed him Karma because if he doesn't like you, karma is a real bitch."

She laughed despite her somber mood. "I can already tell he doesn't like me, so I'll take a couple of steps back to put some distance between us in case he decides he wants to know how I taste. But I'm also turned around in the woods. I haven't been home in a really long time and I would appreciate it if you could see me back to US 87 where my car is parked."

"Not a problem. Karma and I would be happy to walk with you."

She shot a glance toward his dog and shook her head. "I'd like to stay as far away from him as possible."

"Why is that? He can be scary at first, but he's a good dog."

"Considering the fact he's done nothing but growl at me, I'd rather not risk a bite," she hedged.

"If Karma didn't like you, we wouldn't be standing here having this conversation right now," he chuckled. Levi turned in the opposite direction she would've gone without his navigation help. "This way."

2

Levi may not have remembered Ensley Cartier, but he had heard about her case. Deaths, especially those involving teens, were rare in Cattle Cove. Most of the crime that occurred came from the big city when murderers drove out to the country to dump a body in a cornfield.

If Ensley had been this stunning, Levi was damn certain he would've remembered her. But then, based on what she'd told him already, they were six years apart in age. Six years was a huge difference in high school. But comparing someone who was in their mid to late twenties versus early thirties, the age gap shrunk considerably.

Ten years ago when her brother died, Ensley would've been a senior in high school. Levi's chest squeezed for her pain—pain that was still evidenced today. There was something haunted in her eyes that Levi could relate to on a primal level.

Although he had already signed up to serve his country as a Marine, the news about Cooper Cartier and the others had traveled across the miles.

And he could sense her heartbreak even after all these years.

Levi managed to get her back to her vehicle within minutes. It helped this area backed up to McGannon property. He knew his family's land like the back of his hand.

"Thank you," she said. "Knowing where you're going makes a huge difference. I feel like I could've wandered around in there all night. It's my fault. I thought I could get to the meadow and back before dark. My bad."

"Well, I'm glad the worst thing you ran into was Karma."

Her thick wheat-colored hair got caught in a breeze and whipped around her face. Large, cobalt blue eyes stared at his dog, causing his chest to take another hit. She was afraid.

Karma was intimidating. In fact, most folks crossed the street and walked on the other side when they saw the two of them coming. Not that Levi minded. Most people would consider him a loner. He spent most of his time on the ranch and preferred it that way.

On closer appraisal, Levi realized Ensley was

shaken up enough to be trembling. Well, now he really did feel bad.

Maybe he could get her talking so she would relax a little bit. He didn't feel right sending her on her way like this. The fact she was alone and facing what had to be terrible memories made him believe she didn't have a support system here in town. He glanced at her ring finger to see if she was married. No band and no tan line.

"I heard your family moved after you graduated high school. Do you mind if I ask what brings you back after all these years?" Levi asked.

"My brother for one." She leaned a slender hip against her sedan. "The other reason is Lowell Whitfield."

Levi arched a brow. "The coroner?"

"That's right. He worked my brother's case. I never believed his findings."

Now that Whitfield was gone, a few of his cases were in question. She must believe her brother's was one of them.

There was something about Ensley Cartier that made Levi want to get to the bottom of the sadness in her blue eyes and now he was even more curious about her. He couldn't pinpoint the reason for his next words, but the question came out anyway.

"Do you want to grab a cup of coffee? I know a place that has the best you've ever tasted."

"Excuse me?" Ensley's surprised reaction almost had Levi thinking the coffee offer was a bad idea.

Levi wrinkled his nose and took in a deep breath. He'd been outside all day...did he smell bad or something?

His ego wasn't used to being bruised if he asked someone out, and this wasn't even for a date. He genuinely felt bad for the woman and her situation. He didn't want to leave her stressed and looking scared.

"I asked if you wanted to grab a coffee." He shrugged his shoulders nonchalantly like he didn't care about the cold shoulder. He glanced around. "I'm not hitting on you, if that's what you're worried about. I just found you wandering around in the woods and figured you could use a friend."

"I have friends," she said defensively before seeming to catch herself. "But I could use an ally. How well do you know Lowell Whitfield's family?"

Now he really did regret the offer. Luckily for him, it didn't seem like she was going to take him up on it.

"Not well enough to matter."

She made a cluck-noise with her tongue. "I don't believe that for a second."

Her arms were folded over her chest, a defensive move. Her chin was down, a protective instinct. Everything about her body language said she was closed off. Most people did that when they felt vulnerable or exposed.

He'd seen it plenty of times while interviewing

people overseas during his time in Kandahar. He'd gotten pretty good at interviewing witnesses; skills he never wanted to have to use again and one of the many reasons he'd returned to Texas and the land he loved after his tour. Working the cattle ranch that his father had built into an empire was all that Levi cared about.

"Believe it or not, I wasn't trying to insult you by asking you out for coffee."

"I didn't think that you were." Her stiff body language said he wasn't making any progress.

And since this fell into the *not his problem* category, he figured he'd tried to do the Good Samaritan thing. It didn't work out. And he probably needed to count his blessings and move on.

So, why was he still standing there?

"Hold on a second." Ensley blew out a sharp breath and her shoulders softened. "I could actually use a friend. The thought of going back to my motel room after this and eating alone isn't exactly the most appealing thing." She had a little hint of sparkle in her eye, like maybe going for coffee with him would give her a chance to pick his brain a little bit.

Oh great. The first person he'd asked out since his last date with April turned out to be a bust. Levi suppressed a chuckle. He wasn't exactly asking out Ensley Cartier. She just seemed too broken to walk away from and too stubborn to admit she needed help. He'd always had a soft spot for anyone in trouble. He glanced down at Karma. Yep, a weakness that had him fighting for the underdog.

"Is there a place that will let him come inside?" She motioned toward Karma.

"There's one I can think of. It's not too far from here. It'd be faster to take my ATV if you don't mind leaving your car."

She glanced around, looking a little bit helpless and a lot confused. Levi was beginning to think he was losing his social skills. A consequence from moving to the outermost part of the family's ranch as far away from the big house as he could build?

He decided to ignore the adorable dimple on her chin as he waited for her answer.

"Is it busy there? I'm not sure I want to be around a lot of people right now," she hedged.

"I can almost guarantee we'll have the place to ourselves."

"I guess it couldn't hurt to leave my car here for a little while. As long as you promise to walk me back." She glanced down at Karma. "And you keep him as far away from me as possible. I don't want to be too readily available if he changes his mind about me and decides I'm a threat."

"Karma?" Levi feigned surprise. "He's a cream puff."

"Well, just make sure that pastry doesn't decide to take my arm off." Her voice was so low that he almost didn't hear it but also so sarcastic that he chuckled out loud.

Finally, someone who seemed to get his sense of humor.

"That wasn't meant to be funny," she quipped, and he realized he'd assessed her too soon.

"I know," he said a little too quickly. He needed to get his defensiveness under control. Well, this was off to a really great start. But then, company had been in short supply lately. He either needed to talk to another human or actually go back up to the big house. As long as his Uncle Donny was still there, Levi preferred to be almost anywhere else.

"How far is this coffee shop from here?"

Levi turned around and caught Ensley's gaze. His heart betrayed him with a little squeeze. He would deal with that later. Right now, he had one question on his mind.

"Trust me?"

"Why should I? I know your brothers and not you specifically. They were good people. Decent. I know you come from a good family."

She'd used the word, *good,* to describe him twice already. This was going well, he mused.

"From an investigator's perspective, I'd be a pretty bad criminal. My dog's DNA is all over this place." He motioned toward a tree and she seemed to get the message. "Your car would lead them to your identity. My dog would lead them to me. If I had anything less than the best of intentions, this wouldn't be the smartest way to go about it."

"I don't know you personally and I have no idea if the fact you come from a good family means you're a decent person. Or if you're the lone, rogue McGannon." She stared him down and he saw a hint of her personality behind those beautiful blues.

Well, Levi really did laugh now. He also noticed she didn't answer his question. "Do you?"

Another sharp breath later, and her shoulders relaxed just enough for him to see that she was going to say yes.

"Good." He reached for her hand and linked their fingers, a big mistake considering the effect their contact had on him. He ignored the electricity shooting up his arm with enough voltage to revive a dead heart. He had news for her and anyone else; that wasn't going to happen any time soon.

He led her to where his ATV was parked.

"Climb on back." He and Karma were a well-rehearsed team when it came to the ATV. Levi bent down and unlatched Karma's leash. The two of them had been checking fences earlier to make sure there were no places cattle could get out when Karma had taken off. He must've heard someone and gotten spooked. Maybe he'd heard Ensley. Only a couple of times in the last few months had he run away and not at all lately. They were making progress on their relationship.

Levi clearly had a lot of work still to do when it came to handling the retired bomb sniffer. Even a year later, he felt like he was still gaining Karma's trust and strengthening their bond.

When he'd first received the dog, he'd had to drive to San Antonio and fill out a mountain of paperwork. It had all been worth it. Taking care of Karma was the best thing Levi ever could've done. It had given him a greater purpose after he'd soured on the fact that the lines between good and evil could be blurred, thanks to his time overseas.

The ATV barely dipped when Ensley took the seat behind him. She leaned far back so they made as little contact as possible. That took some effort on an ATV meant for one.

He glanced behind him to see that her hands were behind her, firmly planted on the seat. He hoped she wouldn't be disappointed when she saw where he was taking her. He'd been honest before—the place they were going had the best coffee in all of Cattle Cove and probably all of southeast Texas. At least in his book anyway.

It was his respite and the place he went to every morning to make fresh coffee before connecting to the morning call. There was a ranch meeting every day at four a.m., rain or shine.

"Where are you taking me?" Ensley asked.

Levi started the engine, turned to the side, and said, "One of my favorite places."

He waited for her to protest but she didn't. He found that he wanted to hear her story and get to know her a little bit better. Chances were she was just cruising through town, staying for a few days and needed a short-term friend. He was up for it.

Levi could admit to being restless lately. Bored.

Maybe it was the bits and pieces of the case and how devastated the community had been that tugged at his heartstrings and made him want to help Ensley. No family should ever have to deal with the loss of a child.

From what he'd heard, Ensley Cartier had been a loving big sister who cared deeply about her younger brother. Folks had said Cooper was seen with his sister more than his parents. From what he remembered, the two had different mothers. Their father had been labeled as a social climber shortly after moving to town.

People in Cattle Cove had a rare ability to see right through bull. Mr. Cartier had seemed to fit the BS bill. He'd moved the family to town and then joined the country club set. That was about as much as Levi remembered about her family.

Being overseas and facing a different enemy had his mind far away from home and things that went on here. Even so, the news of Cooper Cartier and his best friend's death...news that had rocked the community... had made it all the way to Kandahar.

If memory served, Cage McGannon had been

friends with Cooper. Levi's cousin had played on the same sports team and ran in similar circles. So much so, Levi remembered the case had shocked and devastated his much younger cousin.

Levi rode over the terrain, his headlights shining the way. His favorite lake wasn't far away, and he liked the sound of the wind as it whipped through the treetops. A ten-minute ride later, he pulled up to his campsite.

"I thought you said we were going to the best coffee shop around," Ensley said.

"That's not exactly accurate. I said we'd be going to a place to get the best coffee. Nowhere in there did I say it had to be bought."

"Good point." She climbed off the back of the seat and he half expected her to demand to be taken back to her vehicle. Instead, she walked around the campfire and started searching for something.

Levi stood there for a long moment, trying to figure out Ensley Cartier.

"What are you looking for?" He stood there, perplexed.

"A match."

3

As Levi went to work building the small campfire, Ensley noticed there were two logs butted up against each other. Sitting on one would put Levi's back to the water. With that position, no person or thing could sneak up behind him. She took note of the fact he claimed that seat. She figured it was his usual spot.

From the side of the log facing the lake, he produced a metal lockbox. He unlocked it and, once the fire was going, pulled out supplies to boil water. Next, he set up three metal prongs over the fire and hung a small metal teakettle that he filled with bottled water.

"Nice setup." She meant it.

He smiled and it was devastating to her heart.

"I always keep two cups here."

"Do you have a lot of company?" she asked.

"I have all the company I need in Karma." He smiled again and wiggled an eyebrow. He held up the cups. "An heir and a spare just in case something happens to one. Plus, this always ensures I have a clean cup."

It was practical. It was also easy to see that Levi McGannon was resourceful. One look at his muscled body said he could handle himself in almost any situation. He'd had a more casual, easy-going look about him in high school. She wondered if serving in the military was the reason his once-playful eyes had turned more serious. Or maybe it was just growing up in general and realizing that life wasn't always butterflies and rainbows, like she'd once believed as a small child.

Levi handed her a fresh cup of coffee and she took a sip, noting that Karma lay dutifully at his feet.

"The search and rescue volunteers who found my brother threw away the clothes they'd been wearing that day." It was an odd detail to remember, and yet it stuck in her mind so vividly. She'd forgotten plenty of other details about her brother's life. Details she wished she could recall and couldn't. But for some reason, the clothes stuck in her mind after reading an account from one of the volunteers a year after her brother's murder. Or should she say death, like the coroner wanted everyone to believe?

Levi shook his head and issued a sharp sigh.

"It's unfair." He paused. "I know I said it before, but

I couldn't be sorrier for what happened to your brother. I didn't know him myself, but if my cousin liked him then he was a good kid."

Ensley nodded. She appreciated the kind words.

"He would've graduated college this year. In May. It's really strange when I think about what he would be doing now." Cooper would forever be twelve years old in her mind. That was the strange thing about death. It suspended time for the living.

"I can't say I've been through anything like what you have because I haven't. I can only imagine your pain. I do know what it's like to feel frozen in time, though. I was gone overseas for five years and expected everyone here to be the same age as when I left. Turns out, everyone got older." He smiled and his dimples peeked out.

She totally understood what he was saying though. "Did you come home for visits?"

"Nope. I was stationed overseas and I missed my brothers and cousins. I figured coming home would only remind me of what I was missing here. It seemed like the best way to stay focused was to keep my head down and finish out my tour. It was something I'd felt compelled to finish but also realized it wasn't something I'd do for a living."

"Then why go at all?"

"I ask myself that same question sometimes. Don't get me wrong, I couldn't be prouder of serving my country. I was looking for answers that I thought I couldn't find in Cattle Cove."

"Don't take this the wrong way, but I thought all people with your family's money went to find themselves in Europe and stayed in hostels on their parents' dime." She heard how superficial and shallow that sounded, and immediately felt bad for the judgment. "I didn't mean..."

Levi laughed and it broke some of the tension.

"I'm pretty certain from the outside it looks like we're all trust-fund kids. But we weren't made that way and we certainly weren't brought up that way."

"So, you don't stand to inherit any of the family business?" she asked.

"Inherit? Yeah. Someday. But that doesn't stop a person from wanting to make their own way in life. Does that make any sense?"

"Actually, it does. It makes a lot of sense to me. To be honest, I always sort of felt like my dad was looking to ride other people's coattails and I never respected him for it." Her cheeks reddened. "I probably shouldn't have said that out loud."

"We have an uncle that I feel the same way about. He's been all gung-ho to jump onboard the family business now that he gambled away his own inheritance and he's seen how my father made the company even more successful. He wasn't around to put in the hard work to build it, but he sure is here with his hand out because he happens to share the McGannon last name."

"I feel like my dad would sadly fit into that same category. When he and my mom married, neither one had two nickels to rub together. And then my mom worked two jobs to put him through first college and then law school in addition to having a surprise pregnancy." She pointed her finger at herself. "Once he graduated and went to work at a firm handling trusts and wills, he ended up meeting the person who would become my stepmother and Cooper's mother. Guess he decided he'd outgrown mine." She shook her head like she could somehow shake off those thoughts. "But I didn't come here to talk about my mixed-up family."

She lifted her gaze and focused on Levi.

"I want to know more about Lowell Whitfield."

"I'm sorry to tell you that you're not going to get much more from me than a free cup of coffee and good company." He grinned, obviously pleased with his quip. "I'm afraid to disappoint you but I spend most of my time out here and prefer it that way. I've been out of the loop since Karma came to live with me. I thought it would be better for him if we lived out here and I slowly introduced him to people. Turns out, he doesn't like crowds any more than I do. Basically, fewer people talk to me when I'm with him. Since I'm not up on town gossip, all I can tell you is what you already know. Lowell Whitfield passed away."

"Natural causes?"

Levi arched a dark brow. "From what I gather. Why?"

"He frustrated people with some of his rulings. One of them might have decided to even the score." She lifted her gaze to meet Levi's. Every time he looked at her, warmth shot through her body. Doing her best to ignore the sensation, she took another sip of coffee and then lifted the mug. "Thanks for this. Don't let this swell your already big ego but it is the best cup of coffee I've ever had."

She took one more sip before setting the cup down in the dirt near the fire. She stood up. "Now, if you don't mind taking me to my car, I'd like to go."

She waited as Levi studied her for a long moment. She wasn't afraid. In fact, this was the most relaxed she'd been around anyone in longer than she could remember. But if he couldn't help her, there was no use sitting around talking about old times. Especially since they didn't exactly have a shared history other than both of them living in the same town. Him, for his entire life and her until her childhood was taken away.

In fact, this was so not a good idea. She needed to go. But a voice in the back of her head reminded her that she was in town alone. Based on the way she'd been treated her senior year, Ensley felt unwanted and out of place in Cattle Cove.

"Let me put out this fire and we'll be on our way." Levi jumped into action.

She had barely finished the school year when her

father and stepmom announced the family was moving to Tennessee. There, her stepmom had decided to 'get on with her life' and 'start over' by adopting the girl she'd always wanted and never got. Ensley might have been allowed to move with them, but she wasn't permitted to get within five feet of the new baby. Angela had been off limits.

Being back in town was dredging up a painful past —a past Ensley wished she could leave alone and walk away from. She couldn't. Not until there was justice for Cooper.

Levi finished putting out the fire and it plunged them into darkness. It took a few minutes for her eyes to adjust. There were several clouds in the sky, one of which covered the moon. Stars were hard to see, which was unusual in this part of Texas.

Ensley used her phone's flashlight to see in front of her as Levi packed up his supplies.

"Mind if I ask a question?" He stopped momentarily.

"Go ahead." Ensley figured it couldn't hurt.

With the light from this angle, she could see his face clearly and it was evident that he was choosing his words carefully.

"What do you think happened?"

She knew exactly what he was talking about.

"Three pre-teens went camping in that meadow. Two bodies were discovered four days later with slits that were blamed on animals. One person made it out alive and was found almost starved to death with no memory of what happened. My little brother, who I was more like a second mother to than a sister, was one of the bodies that was found. There were three theories about what might've happened. One killed the other before killing himself after a fight." Ensley found herself recounting facts, as if thinking in detached, basic facts could distance her from the heartbreak that they brought.

"Over what? The girl?" he asked.

She nodded before continuing. "Then there was the accidental poisoning theory. But the problem there is that we grew up around ranching families. My brother was familiar with practices and never would've touched something he shouldn't, let alone ingest it. Plus, hello, there were wounds consistent with knife cuts."

"You mentioned something about animals?" His calm, even tone kept her a few notches below panic. It was hard to talk about what had happened, even now. And especially since she never did with anyone. Once the investigation had concluded, her parents said rehashing the past wouldn't bring her brother back. They'd taken everything on face value without questioning the coroner's decision or motives. At seventeen, she hadn't, either. So, basically, no one had stood up for Cooper.

"That's right. The cuts and slashes were blamed on animals." She rolled her eyes.

"I've seen that happen with bodies that have been dumped in fields," he admitted before shooting a glance that made her wonder if he regretted being so blunt.

She couldn't afford to be offended. "Then there was the fight over the girl theory. She was friends with both boys but was Cooper's girlfriend."

"At that age, being boyfriend and girlfriend meant something different than it does in high school and older," he stated.

"Not to investigators."

"So, you don't believe there's a possibility the deaths were accidental," he said.

"No, I don't. I believe the coroner lied and covered up murder in order to give easy answers, or maybe he was bribed. He could've been protecting someone. All I know for certain is that he didn't have my family's best interests at heart."

"My cousin said the deaths were accidental." He caught her stare and held a second too long.

"Is that what he believed?"

"I guess so. He was always an honest kid who has grown up to be an honest man. He would have no reason to lie." Of course, his cousin just might have the wrong information like everyone else.

"Would it be okay if I talked to him? I'd like to circle back and see what he remembers if you think he'd be willing to talk about it." She figured it couldn't hurt to ask.

"I think he was already interviewed. Everyone at the school who knew your brother gave a statement. Can you request a copy of the file?"

"It supposedly doesn't exist." More lies.

"What does that mean?"

"People were interviewed but when I hired a lawyer to get the case file, we were told that it was missing."

His eyebrow shot up. "Did they have any idea what might've happened to it?"

"Apparently not."

"Tell me what happened that night in the woods," he urged.

"Can't. My brother and his best friend are dead, and the only witness can't remember a thing."

"Is it possible she blocked it out?" he asked. "I mean, it must've been horrific for a twelve-year-old girl to witness both of her friends' deaths."

She picked up on the fact that he didn't use the word, *murder.*

"Her name is Oaklynn Stock."

"I know that family." Concern cut lines in his forehead. "They own a goat farm but stick to themselves mostly."

This was the first good news Ensley had heard so far. "Do you have any idea where she is or what she's doing now?"

"That I do know. She still lives on her family's ranch. From what I heard, she doesn't go into town much. I can't say that I've ever seen her."

"But you don't go into town, either." Ensley headed toward the ATV, preferring to let the conversation die right there. She climbed onto the seat and waited for Levi.

He joined her a few moments later, Karma by his side. The ride back was short, and she was grateful. At her car, she pulled out her keys and then pushed the button on the key fob to unlock the doors.

She stopped at the driver's side. "Thanks for the coffee. You were right. It was the best cup I've had, and it was nice to have company."

Most likely, he was one of the last people who would willingly talk to her in Cattle Cove.

"I'm usually around working the ranch. If you need anything, give me a holler." As honest as an offer that was, they both knew she wasn't going to take him up on it. It was obvious that he would be no use to her and her heart gave a traitorous little flip at the thought of never seeing him again.

She waved instead of conjuring up words that wouldn't be heartfelt.

"Ensley," he began. "I hope you find what you're looking for."

"Thanks," she said. "I do, too."

4

E nsley got into her car and turned on the
ignition.

Click. Click. Click.

Of course there'd be something wrong with her car with the way this evening was going. Murphy's Law was no joke and she was being bit by it right now. She was prepared to walk away and now it seemed she needed Levi's help after all. Going into the woods after dark wasn't a mistake Ensley would make twice but running into Levi had stirred up other feelings. Not only were they feelings she didn't have time for, but they were feelings with nowhere to go. Even if he *was* interested, and that was a big *if*, she didn't have the wherewithal to see anything through right now.

Leaving Cattle Cove, as hard as it had been at the time, turned out to be one of the best things for her. In

Tennessee, there weren't reminders of Cooper every-where. There, it had been easier to forget.

Levi, who'd started to walk away, turned around. He stood with his arms crossed over his chest, studying her. Karma paced and seemed agitated by something.

Her heart went out to the dog and she wanted to help if there was any way possible. But from a safe distance.

"Why's he doing that?" She motioned toward Karma.

"Your car."

"Mine specifically?" She had no idea what he could think was wrong with her vehicle.

"No. Generally. He's used to clearing vehicles before anyone gets near them."

Oh. Right. He'd mentioned Karma was a bomb sniffer.

"What can I do?" It was agony watching the poor animal suffer.

"You really want to know?" he asked, and she immediately nodded.

"He looks like he's in pain," she acknowledged. This couldn't be good for him. He looked more than in pain, he seemed distressed. "If there's something I can do to help, name it."

"Open your car door and get out. Open the trunk. Let him search."

She caught on immediately, popped open the trunk using the lever, and was out of the driver's seat in a heartbeat. There was no reason to watch this animal suffer if all she had to do was let him check out her car to remedy the situation.

"Be my guest." She held out her hand as she stepped away from her vehicle.

On Levi's command, Karma went to work. Nose down, he moved with precision and grace through the front of the vehicle, checking under the seat and running his nose along the dash. Levi opened the backseat and she quickly realized it was to create an exit because Karma hopped over the console without so much as touching it with a paw.

He moved through the backseat and then exited. Then, he was onto the trunk before walking the perimeter.

The dog was thorough and fast. She remembered what Levi had said about not wanting to see a bomb sniffer sit down, and despite knowing there was no bomb in her vehicle, she appreciated when Karma returned to Levi's side and stood.

Levi gave a command, she figured it was to direct Karma to lie down because that's exactly what he did. And he looked much better and more at ease.

"Crank the engine again," Levi urged.

She complied and got the same *click, click, click* noises. Since her car was in otherwise perfect working condition, she knew the battery had died. She smacked the flat of her palm against the steering wheel.

What was it about cars? She had an indicator light

for when a tire was low on air, useful but not always dire. Hers seemed to come on whenever there was a rapid change in the weather. But the battery? No one had come up with an indicator light for when the juice was low.

Frustration had the best of her and she knew it.

"It's the battery. Looks like I need a new one." She waved Levi off remembering she could just call for roadside service and get a jump. "There's no need for you to stick around. I have a service to call."

"I don't mind. I can at least keep you company until they arrive. We won't make it too far on my ATV or I'd run to the store and pick up a new one for you." He checked his watch. "Plus, the part store is closed and the nearest big box store is a solid three-hour drive from here."

"Right. The country. I'd forgotten how isolating it could be out here."

Levi got that half smirk on his face again. He seemed to think better of giving the response that first came to mind.

"I have jumper cables at the ranch."

"No need." Ensley dug around in her handbag for her cell phone. She pulled it out and dialed her service.

"How can we help you tonight?" the polite voice on the other end of the line asked.

"Looks like I need a jump start or a tow into town so that I can have my battery replaced." She highly doubted there'd be a car service out here she could rely on. Those were reserved for bigger cities. She'd forgotten the conveniences she was used to in the city wouldn't be common here. No pizza delivery. No grocery service. But there had been a country club and her father had been all about that.

"The nearest tow truck can be to you in twenty minutes," the dispatcher said.

"I'll be right here," she said for lack of something better before ending the call.

"My offer still stands. I wouldn't feel right leaving you out here on the side of the road." Levi walked to the driver's side and leaned his elbows on the opened window. "How long did they say it would take?"

"A hot minute," she admitted.

"Or I could leave Karma here with you if you prefer his company to mine." The sense of humor shining in Levi's eyes only made him more attractive.

"He'd love that, wouldn't he," she teased. The light-hearted comment broke some of the tension that had been docked on her chest. "If it's not too much trouble, I'd appreciate the company if you wouldn't mind sticking around."

To most, the town of Cattle Cove could be a welcoming place. It had one of those quaint town squares and the people were friendly. As she'd driven through earlier, she'd noticed not much had changed. Several antique shops dotted the main square, there was one of the best steakhouses in this part of Texas. It wasn't all highbrow. There was a hotdog stand, a quaint pizza parlor, and because summers in Texas could melt the rubber soles of her flip-flops, a seasonal snow cone shop. Art in the area was mostly southwest. Several well-known bronze sculpture artists either were from there, had spent time there, or their art was on sale in one of the many shops.

There was a candy store, a bank and places to buy clothes. A cozy bed and breakfast along with a movie theater rounded out the square. The streets were made of cobblestone, preserved from the horseback era.

It also highlighted how long the town had existed. There was a western show on Main Street every weekend during summer and a daily cattle walk, a nod to the region's main source of income. Just on the outskirts of Main was a country kennel and boarding facility for use by anyone headed to the small but private airstrip that took them to Houston International Airport and from there, the world.

The town's population hovered around twenty thousand people, give or take.

Unfortunately, not many of those people wanted to see her again.

Ensley's phone rang. It was her service. She answered on the second ring.

"Everything okay?" she asked.

"I apologize, Ms. Cartier. However, our closest tow truck is pre-occupied. The closest one we have to you will be at least two hours away. My apologies for the mix-up."

"Hold on a second. Are you telling me that when you first called me you had somebody who could come in twenty minutes? I'm assuming you used a computer to locate that person and maybe some type of GPS."

"Yes, ma'am. That is correct."

"You're telling me now that you've contacted them and given them the customer name suddenly no one is available for two hours? Does that about sum it up?"

"Yes, ma'am. It does."

Ensley hadn't expected the mayor to roll out the red carpet when he found out she was back in town. But this?

She smacked her flat palm against the steering wheel again.

"I guess I'll wait then."

"Someone will be there as quickly as we can get them there. I apologize again, ma'am."

"I understand. It's not your fault. I appreciate the assistance." That was how Ensley ended the call.

She blinked up at Levi.

"I'm pretty sure you figured out what just happened. There's no reason for you to stick around and waste your whole evening. From what I remember days on the ranch started super early. You and Karma should go home."

Levi didn't budge an inch. In fact, there was so much intensity in his dark eyes that it took her back for a second. She was pretty grateful that stare wasn't directed at her.

"Unbelievable." There was so much disdain in that one word.

She couldn't agree more.

"It is what it is. I didn't exactly expect a parade. That's why I think I was so drawn to stopping off at the meadow on my way to the motel. I wanted to remind myself why I was here."

"Well, we can do better than that. Call her back and tell her that you don't need help anymore."

"I appreciate what you're trying to do but we're not exactly going to make it to the store on that ATV of yours. You said so yourself. I have no choice but to wait this one out. If someone is coming from two hours away, they won't know who I am and it's not *that* terribly long to wait anyway. I'll be fine."

"I have never known someone to say, 'I'll be fine,' and actually mean it. There's no reason for you to sit out here alone on the road with nowhere to go. I'll make a quick call to one of my brothers and they'll be here in a few minutes. I should have thought of that first anyway."

"Don't go to that much trouble. It's really fine. I kind of expected that kind of treatment here." It did remind her once more to watch her back while she was in Cattle Cove.

"I'm not going to try to force help on you. I respect what you're doing and why you're here. I think I understand why this is important to you and I want to help. It really wouldn't be any trouble to call one of my brothers. If you don't want to bother them, there are ranch hands who can be here any time with a pickup truck and a set of cables."

Ensley sat there, weighing her options. She could stay put for the next couple of hours, hoping the next tow truck driver didn't change his mind once he got close to town or get called away for something else. Or, she could accept Levi's help. It seemed silly to sit there under the circumstances and being so close to the meadow caused an icy chill to run down her back. At night, the place was downright scary. She'd already made a bad judgment call in running off half-cocked into the meadow. Refusing Levi's help would be downright stupid.

"Thank you for your hospitality, Levi. If you're absolutely certain it's no trouble and wouldn't keep you from something else you need to be doing, I'd like to accept your offer of help." She had to admit it was nice to be around someone who had her back for a change.

Levi smiled, nodded, and then in the next half-second had his phone out. Based on the conversation, she gathered he was calling a ranch hand. When she really thought about it, that was probably for the best since ranch hands tended to come and go, and no one would be the wiser Levi had been with Ensley Cartier.

She took the opportunity to cancel the service she called for.

She highly doubted it was possible to slip into town under the radar considering someone had already refused her service. She could only hope tomorrow would bring less resistance. She almost laughed out loud on that one. The truth was that she was mounting an uphill battle. Just because Lowell Whitfield had passed away, and there'd been a few questions about how he'd handled some of his cases, didn't mean she would find any easy answers or people willing to cooperate.

Reminding herself of the fact every day would be her marching orders while she remained in Cattle Cove. And yet, the need to get answers and closure outweighed the common sense that tried to convince her she was on a wild goose chase.

Levi finished the call and turned toward her.

"You might want to come on out and lock up. It won't take Travis long to get here. The bunkhouse is closer to this location than the big house. It's the reason I called there instead of home."

She'd misread that situation. Ensley grabbed the baseball cap from the passenger seat and secured it on her head, tucking in as much hair as she could. She kept the brim low enough so she could see but tried to use the cap to hide as much of her face as possible.

She grabbed her belongings next before exiting the driver's side. She pulled her weekend bag from the backseat. She locked up her sedan and prayed that it would still be there in the morning when they could replace the battery.

"I never asked you how long you planned to stick around. From the looks of it, you look like you're only planning on being here for a couple of days." He leaned his hip against her hood.

"I took an indefinite leave from my job. How long I stay depends on the case and how quickly I get answers. This time I have no intention of leaving without finding out what actually happened to my brother. But if you ask me, the faster I get out of here, the better."

Headlights cut through the darkness.

"That was fast." Levi checked his watch.

Her eyes had long ago adjusted to the darkness considering there were no streetlights on this stretch of road.

Early or not, the truck coming toward them was a sight for sore eyes. She had an unexplainable and creepy feeling that she chalked up to being near the meadow. Was it something else, though?

The truck diverted as it neared, aiming right toward her.

Levi jumped into action. He threw his arm around her and in a few steps had maneuvered them both behind her sedan. He gave a command in German to Karma, who rounded the vehicle and ducked low, sticking so close to Levi's side she was surprised Levi didn't trip over the animal.

Before she could get her mind around what was happening, the truck slowed.

Levi stepped out from behind her sedan and the driver ducked down before hitting the gas.

He chased after the truck on foot but was no match for the engine. By the time he returned, he was out of breath, so it took a few seconds for him to get out the words, "No plates."

"As in no license plates?" she asked for clarification. Being ditched by her tow truck driver was one thing, inconvenient but not worrisome. This was downright scary.

"That's right."

5

L evi's gaze skimmed over Ensley, making certain she wasn't injured. Her face was sheet-white, but her chin jutted out with determination, like there was no way in hell she'd let her fears take over. "I got a picture of the truck but without a license plate and it being so dark, I'm not holding my breath that it'll help much."

"That driver was scary. Coming back here was a mistake," she admitted.

Another set of headlights seemed to cause all her muscles to tense. Levi took a step forward, placing himself in between her and the truck heading toward them from the same direction the other one had come a few minutes ago.

This one slowed down before pulling onto the side of the road and parking. Travis jumped out of the driver's seat. He was young, in his early twenties, with a white cowboy hat on and jeans. He wore boots and looked every bit the part of ranch employee.

"Thank you for coming, Travis." Levi shook hands with the ranch hand before introducing him to Ensley, who'd relaxed considerably as soon as she caught on this was a friend.

Ensley made a move toward her weekend bag, but Levi was already on it. Travis made an attempt, too, but Levi waved him off.

"Do you think my car will be safe here?" Ensley asked.

The question was valid after what had happened.

"I can have it towed to the ranch if you'd like. We can get you set up with a battery in the morning." Levi didn't want to overstep his boundaries. He didn't like the idea of leaving it out in the open wherever she was staying, which had to be the motel. Ensley going back there alone and without transportation bothered him. "You're welcome to stay overnight, or we can get you set up with a vehicle to borrow."

When she didn't balk at the idea, he realized how shaken up she most likely was.

"I can stick around here until the tow truck shows." Travis's offer was solid.

"Thanks, but I'd rather have you on the ranch." There was no way Levi would put one of his workers at risk, especially when he couldn't guarantee the driver behind the wheel of the truck wouldn't come back with friends.

"Yes, sir," came the quick response. "I'll take Karma and let him do his thing."

Levi nodded.

Travis opened the cab doors and let Karma take the lead from there. Levi appreciated that his ranch hands were fully onboard with Karma's new life and understood leaving all that training behind would be impossible.

"What do you think about staying over?" Levi asked Ensley.

Her gaze unfocused like she was looking inside herself for an answer. It was the same thing she'd done when he'd asked her to go for coffee. He was grateful she'd said yes because she could've ended up in a real spot otherwise, considering what happened since then.

"That's probably a good idea," she conceded.

Levi walked her over to the truck before placing her bag in the backseat. By the time they got there, Karma was waiting in the middle of the bench seat in the front of the cab and Travis waited in back.

Ensley climbed into the passenger side with leery eyes on Karma.

"He's okay. Aren't you, buddy?" Levi's reassurance was met with a nervous smile from her.

Levi wasn't real sure what had just happened with the truck that had shown up before Travis, but he sure as hell intended to find out.

Ensley Cartier had a right to be in town. She had a right to try to find out if what they'd said about her brother was true. And if not, she had a right to investigate her brother's murder.

His blood still boiled over the fact that the tow truck operator had refused service. He knew exactly who that was and had every intention of paying Andy Whitfield a visit. Lowell Whitfield's nephew ran a tow truck business and the Whitfield family name sure seemed to be turning up a lot in the past couple of hours.

Bullies were not something Levi tolerated. He would never stand aside and watch someone be pushed around or intimidated. If this was any indication of the reception Ensley was about to receive, she needed more than a friend. She needed backup.

Since she seemed completely sane, level-headed even, and he'd never once heard a bad thing about her personally when her family had lived in town all those years ago, he figured she didn't deserve what she was getting.

So, Ensley Cartier just picked up a shadow. Of course, once things settled down he planned to talk to her about his offer of help. For reasons he couldn't explain, he wanted to show her that Cattle Cove wasn't filled with jerks. To prove that in fact the town he loved, the town where he'd grown up, had a reputation for stepping in and helping others in need.

Strangers were welcomed. Residents were cared for by each other. Not that Cattle Cove didn't have its problems. Every town did. Any time thousands of people were thrown together there was bound to be a certain amount of disagreeing and drama.

This town was no different. But the heart of it had always been good. Or so he'd always believed. And it had been a huge part of the reason why he signed up for the military as soon as he could to protect the values of a country he loved.

After he'd served his time, there'd been no other place he'd wanted to return to. This was home. This was a way of life worth protecting and not one where secrets were kept. Secrets and betrayal were like termites. Once they took hold, they festered and destroyed from the inside out.

So, yeah, he was taking this personally. And he tried to convince himself his reaction had nothing to do with the attraction he felt toward Ensley.

"HOLY COW." Ensley's cheeks heated the second she realized she'd said that out loud.

The McGannon property was impressive from the street. She could only imagine what it looked like on the inside. The big house was set way off the street and was a massive two-story with a twelve-foot star of Texas in the center on the second floor.

The façade was cream-colored stone. There was a welcoming feel to the place, despite it being the largest private home she'd ever seen. And that was just from the street.

Turning onto the two-lane drive, they were met with a guard shack and a security gate. There must've been some type of device on the truck because the gate started opening as soon as they turned onto the drive. And then she realized that Levi had dropped his right hand and pressed a button underneath the dash.

He nodded and waved to whoever was manning the shack. Whoever it was, he looked fresh from the military and capable of taking on any security threat that might come his way. His tense expression softened the minute he saw Levi in the driver's seat.

Levi's wave was met with a salute. Despite it being nighttime, the grounds were well lit which occurred to her was most likely a security measure. It was a lot more difficult to hide in the light than it was in the dark.

Massive oaks stood sentinel on either side of the two-lane driveway. To the left, an even bigger tree held a tire swing. To her right was just a massive front lawn with nothing but grass. Off to one side, there was a firepit with around a dozen Adirondack chairs circling it.

Next to a two-story stone building was a parking lot. It easily fit eleven vehicles. The spots were large enough for any of those vehicles to be trucks and many of them were.

She counted three trucks, two SUVs, and a sedan.

She figured a smaller car was probably not as useful on a cattle ranch. Levi parked and all three of them immediately exited the vehicle along with Karma.

Ensley turned toward the back seat to retrieve her bag but Travis already had it out and in hand.

"I can take that from you." Rather than hand over the bag, Travis looked to Levi. She wasn't insulted. She understood this was Travis trying to be courteous and respectful to his boss.

Levi's nod was almost imperceptible, but Travis handed over the bag.

Ensley tightened her grip on the handle of her weekender as Travis excused himself. She headed toward the massive house as Levi's strong hand splayed across the small of her back. The notion struck that it should feel odd for him to touch her and not like the most natural thing. Despite the heavy circumstances and the awful moment in the woods before he and Karma had arrived, being with Levi felt right.

Because she was home. If she'd met him in Tennessee, she wouldn't have the same reaction. Granted, there was no state line that could make him less hot. Physical contact brought on all kinds of electrical impulses—impulses she should've felt in past relationships but hadn't. Deep down, she had a sense this was different. Special?

There wasn't much to compare it to. Her past relationships had included a handful of boyfriends she could easily walk away from. She'd convinced herself there was a shortage of good men even though that was probably being harsh.

The problem was her. She could only go so far emotionally before she mentally slipped on her running shoes and headed for the door. The last boyfriend, Clark, had stated plainly what the others had only ever hinted at. He'd said, "You know, it's really hard to get to know someone who never stands still. You've had your running shoes ready since our first date. I overlooked it at first. I thought I'd be different... worth sticking around for." The sadness in his eyes had almost made her turn around and offer to give the relationship one more chance. Until he'd added, "You're too selfish to ever let that happen. And I would've been the best thing that had ever happened to you if you would've let me in."

Ensley knew he spoke those words out of hurt, but the emphasis he'd placed on the idea that everything had gone wrong in their relationship because of her hadn't sat well.

Clark had been a decent guy, just not the one for her. His comments had made her realize that she'd only been dating men who wouldn't expect too much from her. Clark represented every guy she'd been involved with her entire twenties so far to varying degrees. And the degrees weren't getting better.

Being alone was best and especially right now. Between the surprising news that came with the coroner's death and the tenth anniversary of losing her brother, the chance to put away the ghost that had haunted her far too long had been too tempting to pass up. Anything else would just have to wait.

"I thought you might be more comfortable if we stayed in the big house tonight." Levi's masculine voice cut through her heavy thoughts. "There's a guest suite on the main floor."

With his hand still on the small of her back, he guided her toward the back door. Even his lightest touch sent her heart freefalling and electricity rocketing through her body. Warmth enveloped her and she had the overwhelming feeling that she was right where she belonged.

Behind the house to the left sat an impressive set of barns. On the right was an even bigger pen for cattle.

"What time does your workday start?" she asked.

"Four o'clock."

"In the morning?" She couldn't possibly have heard him right. "I knew ranchers got up early, but that's intense."

"It was a little rough in my teenage years, especially when I played sports and worked the ranch. I can be honest about that."

"I bet. This place is beautiful and...impressive. Seems like a great place to grow up."

"It was." For someone as obviously wealthy as Levi and his family had to be, the McGannons had always been the nicest and most down-to-earth people. It was one of the qualities she'd admired most about the family. Their humility was the opposite of her own father, who'd been all flash and show. He wore an expensive watch and drove a pricy sports car, and was fixated to the point of obsession about appearances. The family always dressed in their best for Sunday brunch at the country club, and the kids always had to go with smiles on their faces.

She'd seen the unpaid bills pile up and had overheard her father negotiating on the phone with collectors. But every Sunday, the family piled up in the SUV and had brunch at the country club, looking like nothing was wrong.

Ensley and Cooper had been good kids. The reminders to sit still and smile through unbearably long lunches hadn't been necessary. Not even through Cooper's early middle school years when hormones caused him to roll his eyes as soon as their father's weekly pre-Sunday brunch lecture started.

The two would pass a knowing glance and Cooper's eyes would practically roll back in his head. He had a dramatic way that made her laugh, but she'd had to stuff it inside. Humor wasn't something her father could appreciate.

"Don't you live on the outskirts of the property?" she asked.

"I have been since taking on Karma. He does best when he's not around people." The way Levi seemed all too ready to ditch people for a dog, granted a dog in need, had her wondering if there wasn't a more personal story there. Levi had talked about the town like he loved it, but she couldn't help notice he appeared to keep himself separate from the way of life he seemed intent to protect.

But she was beginning to feel a bond with Karma. His need to be alone was the first trait in him she could whole-heartedly relate to. Between that and the lost look in his eyes, the animal was quickly growing on her. Besides, it was his teeth that scared her.

"There's a suite on the ground floor with a couple of rooms. I thought I'd stay across the hall in case you needed something in the middle of the night." He seemed to hear how that sounded when his dark eyes widened and his face broke into a cocky grin. "I didn't mean that the way it came out."

She laughed. It was genuine and the kind that bubbled up from somewhere low in her stomach. It was nice to break up some of the tension she'd been feeling. As it was, her shoulder muscles were so tight someone could probably crack a diamond if they hit it hard enough.

"I'd like that, actually. I'm pretty certain I'd get lost if I tried to find any room in this massive house. And, in case you decide to sleep in, I don't want to scare your family."

Levi smiled as he walked her through a massive kitchen. One wall was basically a wall of every kind of oven imaginable. There was a wood-fired stove in the corner. The paint hues could best be described as light and warm. The place was something she could see the famous Texas designer couple who lived north of there designing. It had that modern farmhouse feel that made her think of big family gatherings on the holidays with cookies baking and lots of laughter.

He cut through the room and down a massive hallway. Inside the house was just as impressive. There were three doors on each side and the hallway lit up just in front of them as they walked. Levi stopped in front of a door.

"I'll let you get settled in and then I'll be back to check on you in a couple of minutes." He stepped aside to allow entry.

Thank you didn't begin to cover the appreciation she felt for what he was doing for her but it was a good place to start. "I really appreciate all your help tonight."

He waved her off like it was nothing before reaching in and flipping on a light. He nodded toward the door opposite hers. "I'll be in there if you need me."

He walked across the hall with Karma at his side. The two looked so at ease with each other. She thought about what he was doing for the dog. Dealing with Karma's issues would frustrate a lot of people. It didn't seem to bother Levi. It was easy to see that he was good with animals. He had a way with them. Sizzling chemistry aside, there was something about his calm demeanor that drew her to him even more.

Stepping inside her room, she was immediately taken back. There was a large four-poster anchoring the room made of solid wood that looked hand-carved. There were two other doors. She went to the nearest one and discovered a nice-sized closet. It was empty of clothes but there were a couple of blankets in varying thickness, folded, along with extra pillows stacked on top.

She wheeled her bag next to a chaise lounge that was positioned near the bed. Next, she walked to the opposite door. It was the one farthest away. She opened it and flipped on the light to reveal a nice-sized en suite bathroom. Everything she could need was there, including a clawfoot tub. In fact, the guest bath at the McGannon home was about double the size of her own and felt more like a spa.

Again, she was struck by how down-to-earth Levi was despite growing up with everything a person could want. Growing up in a place like this, it would be easy to walk around like they owned the place in school.

Granted, they'd been popular but that had more to do with their athleticism and overall hotness. Most of them were decent students. They were what most would consider the total package. Plus, they had that whole carved-from-granite jawline and hawk-like nose with near-perfect bods bit down.

In her humble opinion, Levi was by far the most attractive McGannon. There was something magnetic about him. The draw to him was hard to explain. He had the kind of spark that drew moths to flames. She tried to convince herself the attraction was simple biology. He'd shown up at just the right time in the meadow to save her from whatever was lurking there.

She'd been shaken up enough to accept his offer to stay over, not wanting to be stuck at the motel with no transportation after her car battery had died.

But she couldn't ignore the fact that she'd had a crush on him years ago. A teen's crush but it had been intense. She was an adult now. Crushes were for that young girl she'd once been.

What she felt now toward Levi McGannon was a full-blown attraction. She shook off the unholy thoughts trying to creep in about what she'd like to do with Levi alone in the bedroom.

Instead of going down that road, she refocused on the bathroom cabinets. She opened the first drawer to reveal many items a guest might need during a stay. There were toothbrushes and a fresh tube of toothpaste. She opened a cabinet to reveal a brush and hairspray. There was shaving cream, a razor and deodorant.

They really had thought of everything. It reminded her that Levi was helping out of a sense of duty and not because she was special. He would go out of his way for any stranger or, heck, animal in need. That was just his way.

So, why did that make her chest deflate when she'd been convinced she didn't *do* needing anyone?

6

Once Ensley had freshened up, she stopped long enough to catch a really good look at herself in the mirror. She should be going on vacation with those bags under her eyes. Her hair was a hot mess. She revisited the cabinet that held a brush, and ran it through her unruly mane.

Everyone wanted curls who didn't have them. Curly-haired girls always wanted straight hair. She smiled. Grass was always greener on the other side. She'd managed to wrangle hers enough to look like waves instead of kinks. And that was progress.

On a hook behind the door, two robes were hanging. She retrieved her pajamas from her weekend bag and changed, grabbing one of the softest robes she'd ever experienced. Was everything at the ranch so elegant?

By the time she returned to the bedroom there was a soft knock at the door.

"Come in." She moved to the foot of the bed near the chaise as Levi opened the door and then stepped inside.

For a split second, she saw an emotion pass behind his eyes she couldn't quite pinpoint. Could it have been desire? A part of her really hoped so.

She watched as Levi took in a breath. A small smile tugged at the corners of his mouth—and it was a gorgeous mouth at that. He cleared his throat, relaxed his shoulders and his easy-going demeanor returned.

But hold on a hot second. Had she actually affected Levi McGannon?

For years she'd walked down the street right past him when she was younger and never once had he given her second look. Rightfully so, considering the age difference back then. Fast forward a decade and the years between them seemed like nothing. Was it wrong that she was secretly satisfied that she could get a reaction from him?

She'd gone on to date a few boys, then men, not really thinking much about Levi. He'd been shoved aside in her memories, overshadowed by a tragedy. What the tragedy took from her, time would've stolen anyway. Seriously, who remembered the person they'd had a crush on when they were twelve and especially after moving out of town?

Names maybe. But even that was a stretch at that

age given the distance.

Levi crossed the room holding a laptop that had been tucked underneath his arm. His boots were off and his jeans hung low on his hips. The guy should have been a model instead of a rancher. But then, the fact he didn't seem to realize or care how staggeringly hot he was made him that much more appealing. Her body was keenly aware of the male presence in the room.

"Why did they go out there that night? And why were they alone?" His question grounded her.

She shrugged. "Cooper's birthday was in a couple of days. Oaklynn said she was sleeping over at Alison's. The boys each said they were sleeping over at the other one's house. They carried with them a small tent that belonged to my family and sleeping bags."

"Didn't someone drive them?"

She was already shaking her head. "No, they said they'd meet up at the park. The one on Fitzhugh and First Avenue."

"I know that one. It's a popular place." He made a noise. "Town kids used to meet up at that park for sleepovers back when I was in high school."

"Which is why I didn't think anything about it when I told him to go. I convinced Stella to let him go. She never liked him to sleep over at anyone's house, so Cooper came through me."

"He also must've realized you wouldn't ask as many questions."

She nodded, and then swallowed in an attempt to ease her dry mouth. Her body trembled and her stomach clenched. Guilt was a physical punch.

"You couldn't have known." Levi's quiet reassurance washed over her and through her.

"I wish I could go back." A sob threatened and Ensley stopped right there. Tears wouldn't bring her brother back. If they could, that would have already happened because she'd cried her eyes dry after seeing him, lifeless, like he was asleep or something. Gone was a better word.

"Don't do that to yourself." His warning came too late. About ten years too late in her estimation. She'd been blaming herself since day one.

Overhearing her stepmom ask her father if there was a relative on Ensley's mother side of the family who would take her so they could move away and make a fresh start hadn't helped matters. Hearing her father apologize on her behalf and then tell his wife that he doubted anyone would take her since she was so close to becoming an adult had felt like knife stabs in an already open wound.

Nope. Her parents weren't exactly what she'd call supportive. She'd forgiven them, realizing they were dealing with their grief in the best way they knew how. She'd convinced herself that her father had stood up for her in some small way.

Anything else was unthinkable.

"So, we know they were in the woods and we know

they were all three together. Three best friends. One relationship had developed into something more." She needed to redirect her thoughts and get back on track.

"I heard something about a love triangle," he said.

"That's not right. I don't know how to prove it, but no one's come up with any evidence that was true." Teenagers with a crush weren't exactly subtle. There would've been some indication. Hearts with their initials scribbled in a notebook or diary.

"What else could've happened?" he asked.

"I have more questions than answers there. Could someone have found them? Or did someone know about their plans?"

"The answer to that seems obvious." Levi opened the laptop. "I'm sorry for this next question but it has to be asked. Were they tortured?"

"The cuts on my brother's and Greyson's throats... they were the same." Even now, it was difficult to distance herself and talk about the details.

"Were there any other *deaths* like that in Texas afterward?" he asked, absently stroking Karma's fur.

"None that I know of. The other marks on their bodies were said to have been from the same animal." She appreciated Levi's tact. "But they couldn't be."

"Are you suggesting some kind of sadistic ritual killing?" he asked.

"There were other theories. Every half-cocked philosophy had been fair game. So, yes, ritualistic killing came up. Others believed it was a ghost. Some contended a prisoner had escaped from Huntsville. At least one theory had to do with an escaped mental patient."

"Rumors those woods are haunted have been around forever," Levi confided.

"Which didn't help."

"Couldn't have," he agreed.

"What did others think of my brother?" She wanted to know from Levi's perspective. If anyone had been mean to Cooper, he most likely would've kept it to himself.

"That he was a good kid and a really good soccer player."

She nodded. That, he was. "What about parents?"

Her stepmom, Cooper's mother, didn't know him as well as she did. For instance, he hated scrambled eggs, but she'd made them for him anyway. Every morning. She'd say he needed the protein. Cooper liked eggs over medium on a bagel with slices of ham and cheese.

And the picture that Stella had blown up and put on a stand in front of his coffin—the one with him wearing the tie Stella had forced him to wear every Sunday for brunch at the country club—he would've hated that.

His favorite was the one Henry Murphy Jr.'s dad had taken during a game. Mr. Murphy had captured the kick Cooper got off to score the winning goal causing the team to end the season undefeated. He'd pretended like the picture was no big deal, but Ensley couldn't count the number of times she'd walked past the living room and caught him staring at it, smiling, before quickly returning it to the inside of the top of a stack of books. Stella kept the photo tucked away in a book about gardening despite the fact she couldn't keep a houseplant alive.

That was the picture Cooper had looked at and smiled when he thought no one was around. When Ensley had brought the subject up with her stepmom before the funeral, Stella had blown like a kettle full of water that had been sitting on the stove too long.

LEVI WATCHED as Ensley seemed deep in thought. His fear was that she was heading down a rabbit hole of despair.

"Come over here. I want to show you something." Levi patted the seat beside him.

Ensley moved over and took the spot as he pulled up the photo he'd taken earlier and then uploaded to his cloud storage.

"See that?" He pointed to the far right corner of the truck's back window. The screen on his phone was too small for him to be able to pick up details on the scene. He'd wanted to blow it up as soon as he'd gotten home.

"A sticker?" she asked.

"Looks like there used to be one there."

"Someone must've torn that off in a hurry," she

said.

"It looks that way."

"What do you make of it?" she asked.

"It's a popular sticker. It's not uncommon in these parts and represents a popular brand of farming equipment. It doesn't tell us who was responsible for the run-in, but it'll help us figure it out when we find our guy."

"A black truck in these parts is common," she said.

He nodded. "The color is not going to help us. Put them both together and we'll get closer."

Ensley gasped. "Do you think that person was *the* person?"

"He's connected. I have no idea how but I plan to find out starting first thing in the morning by interviewing Andy Whitfield." Levi knew people took care of their own in Cattle Cove. Would someone cross the line in a legal matter to protect a friend? "He seems like a good place to start. If his uncle is guilty of tampering with evidence, he may know about it, or he may do anything to protect family. Also, he was one of the only people who knew where you were at the time you called in to book the tow truck."

She stared at him for a long moment and he could almost see the wheels turning in the back of her mind.

"I never got a chance to speak to Oaklynn. I'd like to hear from her what happened," she finally said.

Ensley had to know that was a long shot.

"We can try." He didn't want to give her false hope.

The last he'd heard Oaklynn's mother had moved away and Oaklynn had a very protective father. She also had a slightly older brother who Levi had never really cared for much.

"Unless Lowell Whitfield covered for someone else, what would he have to gain by tampering with evidence or covering up the details of your brother's murder?"

"The sheriff had been up for re-election that year. Unsolved crime and especially one as heinous as this one wouldn't be good for campaign purposes. Blaming the boys wrapped up the case nice and neat. Two pre-teen hormonal boys get into a fight over a girl and kill each other. Or one kills his friend and then turns the knife on himself. The only thing missing from that fabrication is a bow."

"And a murder weapon. I'm still surprised people bought that story. I was already overseas and I know how traumatized everyone was by the loss of life and especially with such young people. Fundamentally, I heard all three were good kids," Levi said.

"People wanted closure. They wanted the deaths to make sense. The sheriff fed the community a nice, neat story and then everyone could move on with their lives."

"Everyone except the people who mattered...the victim's families."

A half laugh, half sigh slipped out. "My family wanted to run away. They figured this put a blight on us. We'd be labeled as unlucky. That's what people say when a kid dies."

Levi didn't buy the pre-teen hormone explanation. He and his brothers had gone through puberty along with everyone else in town over a certain age. They all managed to stay alive. But, man, his heart took a hit at the impact that leaving everything familiar, everything she'd come to know and love must've had on Ensley at that age. All his protective instincts flared, and he wished like hell he could go back in time and find a way to right this wrong.

"I knew my baby brother. He didn't own a knife and neither did Greyson. Neither house had any missing cutlery. The whole theory is absurd and still doesn't explain why Oaklynn was found three days later, starved and dehydrated. She was babbling incoherently."

"Dehydration can explain her confusion at the time. What did she say happened?"

"That she doesn't remember anything."

"It's possible she blocked it out." Levi had heard of traumatic situations where a grown adult had blocked out details of an event. He could only imagine what this might do to a developing brain. Panic might have shut her down.

He'd been involved in a car crash not long after he got his license. One of the varsity football players had run a stop sign and T-boned him at the intersection of a drive-in fast food hangout. It was the kind of old-

fashioned burger place people still wore roller skates
to deliver food to a car.

There'd been a dozen witnesses to the accident and
a dozen different stories of what had happened. Levi
learned that day witnesses couldn't be trusted.

Levi stared at the picture of the truck. This close,
he could breathe in Ensley's clean and citrusy scent.
He could also smell peppermint toothpaste and had
never wanted to taste it so badly. He also reminded
himself that he didn't need to be noticing these things
about her.

This seemed like a good time to remind himself
that she was breezing through town and would be
gone the minute she had her answers. Besides, he
wasn't in the best situation to add anyone to his life.
Karma deserved Levi's full attention. And, living on the
outskirts suited Levi better than he should probably
admit.

It wasn't until her that he'd wanted to come back to
the big house at all. Ever since his Uncle Donny had
moved back last year, Levi wasn't in the mood to be
home.

His father had welcomed Uncle Donny with open
arms, a move Donny's sons hadn't been inclined to
follow. How anyone could blow through the kind of
inheritance the two brothers had received was beyond
Levi.

Clive McGannon had stuck around and worked the
ranch when he could've sold and retired. The

McGannon name meant something to him. Unlike Uncle Donny who only seemed to like the family name when he could cash in on it.

Still, Levi could relate to his father's need to protect his younger brother. He'd done the same thing for his siblings and still was.

In Texas, a successful ranch meant the owners had claim to the mineral rights on their land. They did. On top of it, though, McGannon Herd was one of the few highly profitable cattle ranches and that had everything to do with Clive's business sense.

There'd always been something about Uncle Donny that had rubbed Levi the wrong way. Not the least of which was the fact he'd seemed more than happy to dump his five sons on his brother and sister-in-law years ago when his own wife had taken off.

Ensley, who had been studying the picture on his laptop, broke the silence. "Most people think what happened to my family, Greyson's and Oaklynn's was sheer bad luck."

Uncle Donny being back in Cattle Cove was bad luck. Bad luck was something Levi could relate to. What had happened to Ensley's family fell into a whole different category.

"I don't believe that for a second." Levi closed the laptop and pushed to standing. He walked across the room, stopping at the door with Karma at his side. Before leaving, he turned around.

"You're welcome to leave the door open or closed.

However you like it is fine. I'm across the hall and mine will be open in case you need anything. I sent a text to Miss Penny to let her know you're staying over. She's been taking care of us and McGannon business for a long time. It's important for her to know you're here considering she's the one you'd most likely bump into in the hallway or in the kitchen."

"Thank you, Levi. I know those words don't begin to cover what you've done for me—"

He waved her off. "We take care of our own around here, remember?"

She had a lost quality in her eyes that knocked the wind out of him. His hands fisted at his sides. He flexed and released his fingers a couple of times, trying to work off some of the tension that was building. He was gutted and wanted nothing more than to haul her against his chest and tell her everything would be okay.

"I'm serious. I'm not sure where I'd be tonight without you and Karma." She looked affectionately toward his dog. "I appreciate everything you're doing for me."

"It's nothing anyone else wouldn't do." He fought against the urge to tell her how much more he wished he could do. How much better he wanted to be for her as she navigated reliving her family's worst nightmare.

The words she said next would stick in his craw for a long time.

"I highly doubt that. At least not for me."

7

E nsley woke with a start. The sun was up and it took a second for her to get her bearings. Four-poster bed. Chaise lounge. Massive house.

Right. She was at Levi McGannon's ranch.

She stretched her arms as far as she could. Sunlight was peeking through the mini blinds. A quick glance at the clock told her it was half past seven.

Sitting up, she rubbed blurry eyes and bit back a yawn. She'd gotten a little too comfortable in the guest room.

Sliding off the covers, she pushed off the mattress to get out of bed. She freshened up in the bathroom before throwing on a pair of pink shorts with a mint green button-down shirt.

She checked her phone. The battery was low. She'd forgotten to charge it last night. She pulled out the charger from her bag and then plugged it in, figuring it wouldn't take too long to get a good charge going.

Sitting on her bed, she debated what her next move should be. Who she should interview. Being back in Cattle Cove was proving to be more daunting than she originally thought it would be. As much as Ensley wasn't looking forward to the task ahead, it didn't matter. She'd made it here and had no plans to turn back now.

Reaching in her purse, she pulled out a small journal. She'd tucked the photo of Cooper in it. His favorite one, the one where he'd been kicking the goal. He'd been so young and so full of energy. His sandy-blond hair and blue eyes would've given him that California beach look had he lived long enough to hit the waves. He'd had perpetually tanned skin from practically living outside.

But he was frozen, frozen in time. Cooper would always be twelve, almost thirteen in her eyes.

The unfairness slammed into her, fueling her. She opened the journal to the middle and wrote down today's date, followed by the description of the truck and the mostly torn-off window sticker.

A few of the residents of Cattle Cove might refuse to have anything to do with her. At least, she hoped it was only a few. But, Levi had proven to be just the opposite. He was quick to offer a hand up when she'd needed it. Twice. He gave her hope there might be others who were willing to speak to her.

She thought about her car and wondered if someone had tampered with the battery cables. Now that she thought about it, the possibility made sense. She made another note next to the date. *Is someone trying to scare me away?*

She wrote down Andy Whitfield's name and then Lowell's. She drew a line from uncle to nephew.

Underneath Andy Whitfield's name, she wrote, *protect?* Below that, she wrote, *murder.* It would be very interesting to find out what kind of vehicle Andy Whitfield drove.

Her stomach growled, reminding her it had been more than twelve hours since her last meal. Since she figured Levi was already awake, she tucked the photo back into her journal and snapped the rubber band around it to keep it secure. She tucked the pad back into her handbag and then checked the battery indicator on her phone.

It needed more time.

Besides, breakfast and coffee sounded pretty amazing about then; she could pick up her phone after her and the device had refueled. She pushed off the bed and walked to her door. Opening it, she noticed Levi's was ajar. A thought struck that she didn't want to end up alone in a hallway with Karma. As much as she appreciated the animal, and she did, being alone with him didn't seem like the best play.

But then she remembered Karma was literally always at Levi's side and she realized that was most likely part of the training that had been ingrained in him during his time in the military.

Rather than startle the dog, she stepped into the hallway and called out to Levi. She waited for an answer, but none came. On closer appraisal, she saw a yellow sticky note on his door.

The note read: *In the kitchen.*

Well, that was easy enough to find. The kitchen was the only other room she knew.

Retracing her steps from last night, she was surprised to find it so quiet in the house. Then, she remembered how early ranchers got up and figured everyone was out working.

As she neared the kitchen, she heard the familiar click-click-click of the keyboard. Again, she didn't want to surprise anyone and especially one of the military's finest animals, so she cleared her throat.

"Good morning." Levi looked up as she entered the room. He looked good sitting there in a plain black t-shirt and jeans and her body had a visceral reaction to his presence. The cotton material stretched over a broad chest as he stood up. Karma, ever at attention, stood with his new handler. Owner wasn't the right word for the relationship the two of them had. Partner?

The minute she stepped inside the kitchen, Karma's full focus was on her. Ears up, intense black eyes stared at her. She had to give it to him. He was intimidating. And loyal. She was also impressed with the fact that Levi had only had the animal for a year and had made this much progress. It couldn't have been easy to gain Karma's trust.

Levi issued a command in German that she didn't understand, and Karma made a circle before returning to Levi's side and lying down.

"Good morning." She glanced around the massive kitchen searching for two things, something for breakfast and coffee.

"What sounds good?" Levi had been sitting at a massive wooden table. It was the kind that looked reclaimed and hand-carved. It also sat no less than a dozen people. It was a reminder of just how big his family was. Between his brothers and cousins, it wouldn't be hard to fill every seat. She paused long enough to think about how much food it would take to feed all those hungry teenagers. The McGannon brothers were close in age, as were their cousins. Ensley believed Cooper would eat them out of house and home the year he'd had a growth spurt, and he was nothing in height compared to this family.

"Anything would work as far as food goes. But first, coffee." She was still searching for the machine when she heard Levi chuckle. The low rumble from his chest traveled all over her, settling somewhere low in her belly. Warning bells sounded. Getting too close to him was a bad idea.

She did her best to shake that off. Thinking about how much food Cooper could put down when he put his mind to it brought a smile to her lips. It had been so long since she'd thought about him, about the funny things, about their past.

Like the way she'd noticed when he'd discovered girls. Suddenly, the Jack and Jill bathroom connecting their rooms was where she could find him. Staring into the mirror and fussing with his hair. Before that, he'd always been in the backyard kicking a soccer ball.

Then, one Saturday evening she'd found him inside checking his face for acne. Combing his hair to one side and then the other to see which looked best. It had startled and amused her.

It was nice revisiting those memories for a change. Happier memories.

"Coffeemaker is right this way. If you're anything like me, that takes priority over food." Levi smiled at her. He was right, of course, but she didn't want to think about how much they had in common.

Levi produced a cup in record time. He didn't even have to pour water into anything. She was pretty certain there was an espresso machine mounted into the wall as an appliance, and she appreciated having the steaming brew.

He moved to the fridge next. "I can do anything from an omelet to granola and yogurt. Give me an idea of what you like to eat."

"Yogurt and granola sound like heaven. And if you have a piece of fruit, I'd take that too."

"As a matter of fact, I have an entire bowl." And just to prove it, he produced the largest bowl of fresh cut fruit she'd ever seen that wasn't on a buffet table. "Take a seat. I'll bring everything over."

Ensley looked wearily at Karma, who seemed to be guarding Levi's spot at the table. Levi seemed to catch onto her hesitation when he stopped in the middle of the room, fresh coffee mug in hand. "My bad. I'm not sure if he's ready for that."

Not that she wanted to end up a human dog biscuit, but she figured they would never know if they didn't at least try. He hadn't attacked her in the woods when he could've. So, that gave her a little confidence when it came to her and Karma's relationship.

"You've done an amazing job with him. Maybe I could take a couple of steps and let's see what happens." It felt like the least she could do considering the both of them had done so much for her in the past twelve hours.

Levi eyed her cautiously. "Are you sure about that?"

"One hundred percent."

"Absolutely certain?" It was a valid question.

"I'll just move really slow and let's see what happens. You can't keep him away from other people forever. Eventually, you might need to be away for a few days or go somewhere without him."

Levi cocked his head to the left. She'd noticed he'd done the same thing last night.

"All we can do is try," she said.

Levi nodded, but it was easy to see every muscle in his face had tensed up.

Ensley took in a deep breath. She could do this. She could take a couple of steps toward the dog. How hard could it be?

"Easy does it, boy." She said the words low and slow. Then, she took a step toward him. When Karma didn't launch himself at her, she exhaled. Slowly.

One step at a time. That had been her mantra over the past decade. It had gotten her through some of her worst days. And now, she would take one step at a time to help Karma.

The next step proved too close. Karma's ears went up, his hackles raised and a low growl tore from his throat.

Levi issued a command in German but it didn't seem to help. Ensley froze. She didn't dare move an inch. Move toward him and that might be viewed as aggressive. Take a step back and she might be viewed as prey.

As far as no win situations went, this was clearly at the top of the list.

Levi took a couple of measured steps, closing the distance between him and Karma. She also noticed that Levi had maneuvered himself between her and the animal.

This time, Levi used English. "It's okay, boy. No one is going to hurt you."

Karma was locked onto her. And that seemed so not good. She hoped she hadn't just set his training back.

Levi snapped his fingers and caught the dog's attention. The minute Karma shifted his gaze from her to Levi, a calmness came over him. It was a sight to see, but the visual of Levi seemed to snap the dog back into the present.

She'd take it. She'd take all the progress she could get.

"I apologize," Levi started.

"Don't." She meant it. As far as she was concerned, this was progress. "Has he allowed anyone to get that close to him without you standing right next to him?"

"Not yet. You're the first."

"Well, that makes twice. I mean, he barked at me and scared the bejesus out of me in the woods but he didn't bite. Your voice broke through. He retreated and found you. Now, this. Progress, right?" She could hear the shakiness in her own voice. What she said made logical sense and she meant the words even though her nerves were shot. So much for needing a cup of coffee to get her blood pumping in her veins.

But now, she really needed her cup of comfort. Levi set her mug down on top of the table and knelt down beside Karma. He spoke in low, soothing tones as he stroked the animal's back.

Ensley, slowly and deliberately, walked over to the table, trying to shed the fear that was trying to take hold. She picked up her mug and took a sip, liking the burn on her throat and the dark, earthy taste.

Without making much fuss, she took a seat near

Karma and sipped her coffee like she hadn't just felt like her life might be on the line. Whatever Levi was saying to that animal seemed to be working.

Within a few minutes, Karma's ears were down and he'd relaxed his weight onto the floor, even leaning a little to the left. When Levi seemed certain the dog was okay, he stood up and took the couple of steps to get her breakfast.

He returned, bowls in hand, and placed them on the table. Karma didn't so much as breathe heavily at the fact that Levi had stepped away and left the two of them alone.

"Progress," she said. Levi seemed to understand all the intention and appreciation in that one word.

"Progress," he parroted.

He refilled his cup and reclaimed his seat next to her. She'd wiped out the bowl of granola and yogurt and made a good dent in the bowl of fruit by the time he returned.

She took a deep breath and thought about the day ahead of them. There was more work to be done.

"You mentioned that you wanted to talk to Andy Whitfield today. Is that still the plan?" she asked Levi.

"He's on my list along with a few other names," he said. "I got up early and did some digging."

8

L evi's cell phone buzzed on the table. He leaned over and glanced at the screen. "Travis. I should take this."

He answered on the first ring.

"I'm going to put you on speaker, Travis. Ensley is here."

"Yes, sir."

Levi set the phone in between him and Ensley, and then hit the speaker button. "What did you find?"

"Sir, you're not going to like this one bit. Ms. Cartier's vehicle took some damage last night. I can send a picture if you'd like."

"I would." Levi shifted his gaze to Ensley, whose chin had jutted out. She looked ready for a fight, not ready to roll over. Good. If she wanted to get the answers she was looking for, she was going to have to buck up for a fight. Also, good? She wasn't going to have to do it alone.

They waited a few seconds for Levi's phone to buzz. His smartphone could multitask, so he pulled up the picture without ending the call.

Ensley gasped, and anger shot through Levi's bones the second he saw the picture. Her tires looked like they had been slashed. Someone had taken a can of black spray paint on her white sedan and had written the words, *go away!*

Maybe Karma had it right all along. He'd lost his trust in people and based on what Levi was seeing here, he couldn't say his dog was far off. At least with a few.

"Why would somebody do that?" The shock and horror in her voice would stick with Levi long after she disappeared from his life. Her question was rhetorical. It was obvious someone didn't want her in town. Someone didn't want Ensley digging around with questions. Someone didn't want the truth to come to light.

And yet ruining her car would keep her there. It told him the vandalism might have been a knee-jerk reaction.

"We need to bring the sheriff in," Levi said.

Ensley was already shaking her head before he finished his sentence.

"It's not the same person. Sheriff Skinner retired three years ago. We have much better representation now. I think you'll like her." Even he could admit Skinner hadn't exactly been the best or the brightest. He had, however, been the most political and his family ties had most likely gotten him the job in the first place. Levi had heard his father complain more than once about a sheriff who was too tied to a good ole boy network. Considering crime in Cattle Cove mostly consisted of teen pranks and water disputes, Skinner had been okay for the job.

But this?

This was over the man's head.

Ensley sat there, her hands fisted in her lap. He could only imagine how violated she must feel. Hell, he felt it for her and it wasn't his property that had been vandalized.

"The sheriff we have now might be more willing to reopen the case." Levi had heard nothing but good things about Laney Justice. She'd been a couple of years older than him in school so he didn't know her personally, but the Justice family had always been in good standing. He believed she would be fair.

"I talked to Skinner once as a teenager. He made me feel like we were just an unlucky family." She shook her head. The words came out so quietly he had to strain to hear them. She was louder when she said, "But if you tell me this sheriff is different, I'll give her a try."

Karma seemed to be picking up on the tension. His ears were up and his body tense.

"Who is with you?" Levi asked Travis, thinking he didn't want his employees alone at a site that was clearly being watched.

"I have Lawrence with me. Hawk is aware we are off property, sir." Hawk, the foreman, had gained his nickname because nothing got past him.

"I appreciate you and Lawrence. I'll send someone with a winch. We'll get her vehicle on ranch property. Stay with it until the vehicle gets picked up and, if you don't mind, pick up my ATV. It's not far from here." Levi gave directions. As he hung up, he thought about exactly how much he despised bullies. Sneaking around in the middle of the night on an abandoned car and vandalizing it fell into that category. The spray paint, the threat, hinted at an evil Levi didn't think existed in the town he loved. The cat was out of the bag now.

On second thought, he shouldn't tamper with evidence and neither should Travis or Lawrence. He fired off a text to Travis to make sure neither one touched the vehicle and advised both to stay inside Travis's truck until the sheriff arrived.

"Technically, your vehicle is a crime scene now. At least we can get the sheriff to tow it and get it off the street. She might want to hang onto it as evidence."

Ensley was quiet. Too quiet. A storm was brewing behind those beautiful eyes of hers.

"Might be easier to get the sheriff to reopen the case now." Her voice was the kind of calm that was like looking on top of a lake. The surface was still, but no one could predict exactly what stirred underneath.

"I hope so." He meant every last one of those words. But if the sheriff wouldn't reopen the case, he had ways. At the very least, he intended to hire his own investigator. It wouldn't be as easy or efficient as having a law enforcement official involved, but he had no plans to sit on this or watch Ensley suffer. "I'd like to help you with this case. I'd like to see it through."

Levi was sincere on that point.

Ensley was already shaking her head. "What about Karma? You have to think about him. You have to put his needs first. Taking him around to interview a bunch of strangers or onto a bunch of new properties wouldn't be good for him."

She had a point. But there also came a time when boundaries had to be pushed a little bit. This seemed like one of those.

"You said yourself that he's never going to get better if I don't expose him to different people and places. My last name means a lot in this town and it'll help open doors for you. I'm shocked by what's happened. I'd like to think that kind of evil doesn't exist here, but it's obvious to me now that it does." He paused for a second to let her think about that. "I need to report this crime to the sheriff. She will most likely want us to meet her there so she can get a statement from both of us. Are you up for it?"

Ensley put her palms on the edge of the table and

then pushed to standing. "I'm ready now. I just need to grab my things."

"You can leave your weekend bag here. It's obvious to me that it's not safe for you to stay in the motel alone."

"I won't argue there." She seemed to take a second to consider the gravity of his words. "I'll grab my purse."

Levi drained his coffee cup as she disappeared down the hall. The way this day was shaping up, he'd need all the caffeine he could get.

While she was gone, he made a quick call to the sheriff, briefing her on the situation. Just as he suspected, she wanted to meet at the site. That had been a no-brainer. What he was still scratching his head about was the question of what she might uncover about why Ensley was perceived as a threat.

Whether Levi believed her initially or not, and he had, he was even more convinced something evil lurked beneath the surface of Cattle Cove now.

Vandalizing her car had been a stupid move. Now, he had a good reason to get law enforcement involved.

Levi crossed the kitchen and made a couple of to-go cups filled with fresh brew. He'd already allowed Karma to perform his 'search' of the house, a routine the dog needed to perform to keep his nerves on an even keel. He'd fed and walked his dog. Routine meant everything to Karma and was most likely responsible for the few breakthroughs they'd experienced. And Levi found relief in the daily routine they'd developed.

By the time Ensley returned a few minutes later, Levi had tucked his cell phone in his pocket and had placed a leash on Karma. He nodded toward the counter. "I made a couple of to-go cups in case you're interested."

"Absolutely." She moved to the counter and double fisted the mugs. Within another couple of minutes, Karma had 'cleared' the truck and they were on the road, heading toward the spot where Ensley had left her vehicle.

It dawned on Levi that someone had most likely tampered with the car last night even though he couldn't see anything with the naked eye. Someone had tried to strand her. Then what?

She'd called it in to roadside assistance. Again, small town. Folks talked to each other. If someone had seen her driving in or found out about the call for help, news could've traveled.

It was lucky that he and Karma had been in the woods checking fences on the back side of McGannon property.

"Did you make any stops near town or pass by anyone you recognized on your way in?" he asked.

"I stopped for gas and a bottle of soda off the interstate," she said. "I lived here so long ago and I was so young...a few people seemed familiar but no names came to mind. Most people change in a decade." She flashed eyes at him. "It's been ten years since I was here. It's been too long. Plus, it was off the interstate so I figured it could've been anyone. It's strange, but in coming home I felt like everyone would be the same age as when I left. I guess time moves on even if it freezes in our minds."

Levi had shared a similar sentiment about returning from overseas. He totally got where she was coming from in feeling like the town would've been frozen in time. He knew one thing, nothing stood still forever.

Sheriff Laney Justice's SUV was parked to the side of the road. She'd beaten them there. Levi parked behind Travis's truck and held onto Karma's leash as they exited the vehicle. The leash wasn't Karma's favorite thing. He wasn't used to it, but he was adapting slowly.

This spot was no longer strange to him. He would recognize his own scent from last night. Scent was his specialty. He'd been given the job in the military because of his keen sense of smell. He also acknowledged Travis and Lawrence without much distress. However, when it came to the sheriff, Karma was on alert. It could be a flashback from his days in the military. She had on khaki pants, her radio clipped to her shoulder strap and she wore a holster on her hip.

Levi introduced the sheriff to Ensley, who briefed her on the situation. Sheriff Justice pulled out a small notepad from her front pocket. She was five-feet-two on a good day. Make no mistake about it, she was dynamite, tiny but mighty.

"Well, you already know my name is Ensley Cartier. I parked here last night and had car trouble. The decision was made to leave my vehicle here overnight and this is what we found today."

Sheriff Justice nodded and looked up at Ensley, who had a solid four inches over the sheriff. "What time were you parked here last night?"

"Just before sundown and was here until not long after. I didn't check the time."

"Do you have an approximate guess?" There was no judgment, just a search for facts.

"I was watching the sunset, trying to beat it. I wanted to get to the meadow before the sun went down. I misjudged the time. I was distracted and a little emotional. This is the first time I've been home in ten years."

"Welcome back." Sheriff Justice's words were filled with compassion. Levi hoped that meant Ensley would be able to trust her.

"Thank you. I'm just breezing through. I heard that the coroner passed away and a few questions have come up about past cases. My brother was killed ten years ago in the meadow I was trying to find. His name was Cooper Cartier."

Sheriff Justice was calmly nodding her head. "I'm sorry for your loss, Ms. Cartier."

"I appreciate your sentiment. But I'm here for

answers. And it doesn't seem like someone is real happy that I'm here. The coroner's nephew, who owns the only tow truck company in the area, refused service last night."

"Is that so?" Sheriff Justice's interest seemed piqued.

Levi could almost see the wheels turning in the sheriff's mind.

"A black truck with a partially peeled off sticker on the passenger-side window drove by here last night and almost directly into us." Levi showed the picture he'd taken of the truck. "The driver swerved at the last minute, barely missing us and her vehicle."

"Can you forward that picture to me?" she asked.

"I can do it right now." He did.

"I'd like to take a look at your brother's case for myself. I'm afraid I've only been on the job for the past three years and that happened before my watch. Again, I couldn't be sorrier for your loss." She glanced at the vandalized vehicle. "This isn't normally the kind of welcome folks receive in town. You already know that since you lived here once. We aim to do better than this."

Ensley scraped her top teeth across her bottom lip, and then said, "I'm counting on it, Sheriff."

9

After taking statements, the sheriff offered to have Ensley's vehicle towed when she was finished with it. A call came in and she excused herself to take it. A small seed of hope sprouted in Ensley's chest after meeting Laney Justice. This was the first time she thought her brother's case might have objective eyes on it. She knew better than to put too much stock in the feeling, and yet she didn't want to ignore it.

Since Karma had already 'cleared' the truck once, he didn't have to do it again. As they walked toward it to regroup, Levi said, "I'd rather know who was taking care of your car and I'd rather have it on McGannon property."

"I'd like that. And I'd like to pay for the transfer. How would that work?" Ensley had money saved. She didn't have a family of her own depending on her financially. Covering the cost wouldn't take much out of her savings. She made a mental note to call the insurance adjuster and request a copy of the complaint from the sheriff so she could be reimbursed for repairs.

"We'll figure something out once the sheriff is done with it."

"I don't want to sit around and wait while she gets up to speed on my brother's case. I don't know how much of a priority a ten-year-old cold case will be for her and I'm on a limited time schedule." She didn't add what she really felt, which was her brother had waited long enough for justice to be served.

"Agreed. Time is of the essence and we have no idea where this case falls on Sheriff Justice's priority scale. This incident could be classified as simple vandalism, even though the words written on the side of your vehicle were pointed," he said.

She was glad to hear him say that because she felt the exact same way. "Except for the message directed at me, someone could write this off as teenagers playing a prank."

She hadn't done any of those things in her teenage years and figured teens in general got blamed for a lot of things they didn't do. It was like in school when a couple of kids misbehaved and the whole class had to sit in for recess. Where was the justice in that? Punishing innocent kids as a blanket statement only hurt the good ones. The same thing had happened to

Cooper's case. Sadly, there were teenagers who fought over girls. There were teenagers who got into fights or accidentally killed each other. It happened even though it was rare. But to put a blanket label on all teenagers as reckless or out of control because of hormones was wholly unfair.

If she'd learned anything from this case, it was that people liked easy answers. Anything that required more explanation than a sentence started to lose people.

"Where would you like to start?" Levi asked.

"Lowell Whitfield's nephew seems like a pretty good jumping off point. Why not begin there?"

Levi waved at the sheriff before climbing into the truck with Karma. Ensley took the passenger seat.

A few thoughts ran through Ensley's mind as she and Levi made the drive to Andy Whitfield's property. He lived on the outskirts of town despite his tow truck business being located on Main Street. At this early hour, Andy would most likely be at home. She wanted to catch him before he left for his workplace. Catch him while he was still eating his breakfast.

Ranchers may get up at four o'clock in the morning, but tow truck drivers worked around the clock, and especially at night.

Andy Whitfield lived on an acre of land in a cul-de-sac neighborhood.

"He has three children. All boys. His wife owns a small craft jewelry business that she works at from home." Levi stopped the truck in front of a nice-sized two-story brick home. Ensley appreciated the update. Part of her didn't want to think about him as a human being. She didn't want to acknowledge him as a dad or husband. She didn't want that to soften her stance if she needed to be tough. So, she tucked the information deep inside. She'd gotten really good at tucking away pieces of her. Too good?

Levi gave her a minute before he shut the engine off. "Ready?"

There were so many questions that had been running around in Ensley's mind while she waited for a moment like this to happen. Now, all of a sudden, she was drawing a blank. Her pulse kicked up a few notches and that probably wasn't helping.

Whether her body cooperated or her mind, she was ready to face down Andy Whitfield. At the very least to ask him why an innocent person would refuse tow service to her.

"You bet I am." She'd hesitated a moment ago, but certainty arrived as on time as the rain in spring.

Levi reattached Karma's leash. The dog didn't so much as glance at Ensley. Had he accepted her as part of the pack? He didn't seem to mind her presence as long as Levi was around.

"Hold on a sec." Ensley reached inside her handbag and searched for her journal. She closed her fingers around its soft edges and then pulled it out of her bag. She pressed the journal against her chest in the spot where her heart beat frantically.

She traced her finger on the elastic band that held the pages closed and kept her brother's favorite picture tucked inside. She fanned out the pages until she located Cooper's picture. Seeing him grounded her. It gave her focus.

Levi sat in a respectful silence. When he seemed to think it was okay, he asked, "Is that Cooper?"

"It is. Would you like to see?"

"I would very much like that." Those words sent warmth through her and cracked some of the ice that had formed in her chest. Ensley held the picture out so Levi could see it. The move meant reaching over Karma. If anyone believed dogs weren't perceptive, they had no clue. He seemed to catch onto the somber moment and didn't budge when she met Levi's hand halfway across the cab.

It was probably too soon to drop her hand and pet him but the desire was there. This was a start. Progress.

Ensley sat there in silence as Levi studied the photo.

"He was good," Levi said.

"Soccer was his life until recently..." She caught herself talking about him like that goal had just happened yesterday and he would just show up at any minute. Somewhere in the back of her mind she realized there was no way that was happening. Thinking of him in the present kept him closer to her. "Girls. He started to notice girls and suddenly he was not in the backyard anymore, kicking a ball into a goal post. He wanted to hang out with Greyson and Oaklynn more."

It was so nice to talk about her brother in happier memories. She never did that. She never did that with her father. She never did that with her stepmom. And Stella seemed determined to make the subject of Cooper off limits to now eight-year-old Angela.

"My brother was such a prankster. I don't think most people ever saw that side to him. Certainly not at school. My father would come down hard on us if we stepped out of line, especially in public. It was game over. But if Greyson was over or it was just the two of us, he was always pulling something." It was a strange sensation to want to laugh and cry at the same time. She did.

"The soccer part was most likely how he connected to my cousin, Cage. He's right here in this picture." Levi pointed to a dot, to a face. It was one she recognized because McGannons were pretty unmistakable. Cage's fists were pumped in the air, his huge smile plastered on his face. He beamed. Cooper was about to end their season on a win.

"They both looked so happy," she said. It wouldn't be long before that face was blank, and all the emotion was drained of it.

"I can tell how much you miss your brother. He was lucky to have a big sister like you to look out for him. Not everyone does."

Ensley really did have to fight back the tears welling in her eyes now. "I don't think my parents would agree with you on that front. They won't let me spend time alone with their new daughter. It's like they think I'm going to infect her with something. Like I'm bad luck."

Saying those words out loud were knife jabs straight to the heart. Breathing hurt as she thought about the rejection she'd faced after losing her best friend. They might have been a few years apart but no siblings were closer than her and Cooper. She'd secretly wished for a brother or sister all those times her parents had fought when she was little. She'd wanted a playmate so badly.

After the divorce, she really wished for another kid in the family. Truthfully, she'd hoped for a sister but her mind had changed after Cooper came into the world.

Levi calmly handed over the picture and took a minute to speak like he was choosing his words carefully.

"You know, I never did like your dad. No offense to you. And his wife wasn't any better. They had a reputation for not having a whole lot going on under the surface. He seemed like he came here to take and that's never been the philosophy here. It's never been the philosophy of ranchers. And if he made you feel like that after how much you looked after your little brother, I like him even less now." Those words were balm to a wounded soul.

"I know he's my father but he's not real high on my list of favorite people, either. I will always love him, but respect is earned."

"I couldn't agree with you more. And if he's idiot enough to keep someone like you—someone who is kind and caring, giving and loyal—away from a sibling, then I have no use for him. If those aren't the attributes he's trying to instill in his other daughter, then he doesn't seem like the brightest person to me."

"That means a lot, Levi." The emotions trying to engulf her were building. Break that dam and she had no idea how bad it could be. Open those floodgates and she had no idea what the damage would be. So, she glanced at Andy Whitfield's house. He might be a husband. He might be a father. But he also might be covering up for his uncle. He might have the answers she'd been searching for almost a decade now.

She glanced down at the photo in her hand before placing it inside her journal and then replacing the elastic band. She carefully tucked the small book into her handbag. No words were needed to tell Levi she was ready to speak to Andy Whitfield. He'd already clicked the leash on Karma earlier and those two were exiting the vehicle on the driver's side. She opened her door and climbed out of the passenger seat.

There were no fences around front yards in this

part of town. The backyard had an eight-foot board-on-board privacy fence.

There was one of those massive SUVs parked next to the house. She scanned the area for a black truck. Didn't find one. The SUV was common and especially for families. There were no matching stickers on the back window. She checked for that too.

Nose to the ground, all the signs Karma had snapped back into his training mode were present. She heard Levi offer soothing words to the dog, low and calm. The reassurance might be meant for Karma but it traveled all over her, entering every fiber of her being.

Before they made it onto the porch, the front door of the Whitfield house swung open so hard it smacked against the brick. A very concerned-looking man stepped out. She didn't remember Andy Whitfield from years ago. He was older than her. This had to be him. He wore a cowboy hat, boots, jeans, and a button-down shirt. Heavy clothes for such a hot day. He was on the tall side but still several inches shorter than Levi. Andy Whitfield was lean and looked to be in his early forties, if she had to guess. He had small, beady rat eyes on top of a long, thin nose.

"Andy," Levi started.

The man became agitated, waving his hands like a wild person. "This is private property. You have no right to be here. This is my family home."

Karma's hackles raised and he unleashed a torrent

of barks. He dropped his head low to the ground, and she realized the move was most likely to protect his neck. Whether it was instinct or training, she didn't know. Maybe a combination of the two?

Either way, it looked effective. Andy Whitfield backed up a step. His reaction to her coming to town seemed over the top, even to a town that valued its privacy.

"We just have a couple of questions for you, Andy. What problem could you possibly have with that?" Levi asked.

"You don't have a right to be here. You of all people should know that, Levi. Plus, what did you bring with you...Cujo?"

Ensley figured Andy should be more concerned about her than the dog. "Why did you refuse service to me?"

"I'm not answering that."

"Well, at least you're not denying it. I figured you would at least start there." She was goading him into an argument, figuring it was the best way to make him slip and say something he'd regret. Based on his reaction to them so far, she didn't have a lot of time to get answers out of him before he kicked them off his property.

The man was acting guilty as sin. Obviously, he had something to do with this or something to lose.

"I'll call the sheriff," he threatened.

Levi stopped and smirked, looking like nothing the

man had said so far was bothering him in the least. "Go ahead. Call the sheriff. She's going to drop by anyway. Of course, you could save yourself the trouble and talk to us now."

Andy's rat eyes widened and a look of shock passed over his features.

10

For a man claiming his innocence, Andy Whitfield sure was acting guilty.

"How did you know it was my vehicle?" One glance showed Ensley's hands fisted at her sides and her back ramrod straight. It was easy to see her agitation pulsing off her in waves. "Never mind. You knew it was my vehicle and you knew where it was because of the roadside service that I use. They called you, didn't they?"

Whitfield was shaking his head.

"You do realize that the sheriff is going to drop by for questioning. You're not going to be able to lie about this or cover it up. It's so obvious that you refused service. My contact told me so last night. You can't wiggle your way out of this or refuse to answer the question in court." Ensley's words seemed to anger him even more.

Good.

Levi added, "Skinner isn't around anymore to cover for you."

Those words scored a direct hit. Whitfield seemed taken back. He caught his mistake and recovered quickly with a sneer.

"What happened to your vehicle was probably kids. You know how they are. Teenagers. They probably thought the vehicle was abandoned and came across it while out joyriding. What's the real harm in that?" Levi wanted to knock the self-satisfied smirk off the man's face and Ensley seemed ready to do just that.

In fact, she practically launched herself at the man. Not that Levi wouldn't have enjoyed the show. He would put his money on Ensley any day to come out on top of that fight. But she could be charged with assault and that wouldn't be good for her case.

He stepped in between her and Whitfield as she muttered a few choice words under her breath—the same words Levi was thinking.

Levi backed Ensley up a couple of steps to put a little more space between her and the source of her fury. He gave Karma the command to retreat as a young guy came bounding out the front door.

The kid was tall and lean, a spitting image of his father only skinnier.

"Is there a problem out here, Dad?" The kid looked ready for a fight.

Levi also noticed the kid brought a baseball bat

with him. Smart kid. He seemed to know when they were outmatched and was ready to defend his father.

"Go on back inside the house, Boyd. I'll speak to you when I'm done here."

Whitfield's son looked to be about driving age.

"Let's go," Levi said quietly to Ensley.

Confusion stamped her features. She had questions and desperately wanted answers. The man she believed could give them to her stood fifteen feet away.

Whitfield would sooner drink rattlesnake venom than give her what she wanted. But Levi had already gotten all he needed.

"Trust me." He locked gazes with her. Karma was calm for the moment, barely contained. But now that Whitfield's son had come out the situation was going south fast.

Ensley stood there for a long moment, her back teeth grinding. And then she nodded almost imperceptibly before turning toward the truck.

Stopping a few feet shy of the vehicle, Levi turned. "So, where were you last night, Boyd?"

Boyd opened his mouth to answer. Whitfield shot a warning look.

"Home," Whitfield interjected.

"I hope that's true for your sake."

Once back inside the cab, Ensley turned to Levi. "You picked up on something I didn't. What was it?"

"He busted himself. He acknowledged he knew that your vehicle had been vandalized. According to his statement, he'd been home all night. If he wasn't involved, how would he know what happened?"

Ensley was rocking her head. "That's a good point."

"The sheriff will stop by to question him. We made certain she would if he doesn't call her to report us, which is a possibility."

"If he does, we'll know which side she's on pretty fast," Ensley said. It was easy to see why she wouldn't blindly hand over her trust. Her reaction also made him realize just how much she'd gone out on a limb to trust him last night.

Despite the fact he'd almost convinced himself that he didn't need anyone in his life, Ensley was wiggling her way into his heart.

"True," he agreed. "I'm not plugged in enough to know who Whitfield's close acquaintances are, let alone his friends."

"Speaking of the sheriff, do you think it would do any good to stop by her office and ask to see the case file?" she asked.

"I doubt she'll be ready to hand over details before she has her own bearings."

"Good point."

"We can talk to Greyson's family and then there's Oaklynn's. I've been out of it for the past year and haven't kept up with families in town and..." Levi's ringtone sounded, causing Ensley to take in a sharp breath.

She glanced at him as he pulled over to the side of the road and fished his cell out of his pocket. He checked the screen and then looked to her.

The look in his eyes had the effect of an espresso shot on her system.

"It's the sheriff," he said.

"I can't say that I'm surprised."

"I'll put her on speaker." He took the call and the sheriff's voice filled the cab. "I'm parked and Ensley is here."

"Good," Justice said, her voice was all business. "I want both of you to hear this."

Another look passed between Ensley and Levi. She could guess what this call was going to be about. Andy Whitfield.

"I just got a call from Andy Whitfield. He wants to file trespassing charges against the two of you."

"He's a liar." Levi's voice left no room for doubt.

"I never said he wasn't. That doesn't mean you can go question him." She paused for a few seconds like she wanted that message to sink in. "I'm back at my office and this case gets my full attention today. Give me a minute to unpack what I see here."

"Cooper Cartier has been waiting almost ten years." It was all Levi said. All he had to say.

"I know and that's why I'm giving this case my full attention. I will do everything in my power to find out what happened that night. But, you have to give me a little room and not rile up my witnesses."

Levi glanced over at Ensley. She didn't even realize that her hand was already in her bag, searching for the journal until that moment.

"Andy Whitfield's son looks guilty of something. It might be a good idea to ask him where he was last night," Levi said.

"No offense, Levi, but I'm good at my job."

"Point taken," he conceded. "The only other thing I'll say is that he knew her car had been vandalized. Andy. How did he know that?"

Ensley's pulse raced until her fingers touched the familiar texture of her journal. Her fingers closed around it and she released the breath she'd been holding.

"Give me a few hours. I'll be in touch with questions. Until then, can I count on you to leave things alone?" the sheriff asked.

Levi sat there, white-knuckling the steering wheel. He just sat still, and Ensley appreciated the fact he seemed to be waiting on her to respond.

So, she said, "We can probably take a break long enough to eat lunch."

Ensley had just as much right to ask questions as anyone, probably more so in her book, considering this was her brother's case. She'd also read up on cold cases and learned the more time passed, the more difficult it became to find the killer. Ten years after the fact, the answers she wanted seemed further away than ever.

"I appreciate the leeway, Ms. Cartier."

"Andy Whitfield and his son are guilty of something," Levi reiterated.

"I'll keep that in mind. In the meantime, no more trespassing," Justice warned.

"We'll see what we can do." Ensley wasn't ready to make promises she couldn't keep. She could give Justice a couple of hours.

Levi ended the call and navigated back onto the road. "I'm guessing Greyson's and Oaklynn's families won't exactly be thrilled to see us."

"Both avoided me and my family like the plague after the murders. I doubt anything's changed there and the last thing I want to do is cause Oaklynn any more pain. That kid has been through the ringer." Ensley motioned toward the cup. "My coffee's gone cold. I barely took a sip."

"We could head back to the ranch. I can rustle up some lunch there. It might give us a chance to think things through and do a little more digging. Maybe speak to my cousin or a couple of my brothers closer to Cooper's age." Levi blew out a breath. "Anyone in my family is more likely to be plugged in to the community than I am."

A lightbulb seemed to go off in Levi's mind.

"You know who socializes more than the rest of us.

Miss Penny. She might be the best one to ask who is doing what and where," he said.

"Miss Penny it is."

By the time they reached the ranch, Levi had called to prep Miss Penny for the fact they were coming and were hoping to talk to her. He also contacted his cousin, Cage, to ask him if he was close enough to the house to drop by for lunch. He'd said he was.

Miss Penny was waiting in the kitchen by the time they returned to the big house.

The smell of garlic and fresh vegetables cooking filled the air, reminding Ensley how hungry she was despite the fact she didn't think she'd be able to eat.

Miss Penny looked to be in her mid-to-late sixties. She could best be described as tiny but mighty. She was petite with soft edges and she walked across the kitchen to meet them with a natural skip in her step. Her short salt and pepper hair was feathered to one side.

"Miss Penny, meet Ensley Cartier."

Ensley held out a hand but was quickly pulled into a warm embrace. Miss Penny had the most clear green eyes—eyes that said she saw everything. There was kindness and compassion in them, and just a dash of fire. She had on a flowery blouse with jeans. An apron covered her outfit with four large letters that spelled out the word, BOSS.

Despite being on the small side, Ensley had no doubt the woman could take care of herself. It was easy to see the respect in Levi's eyes.

Miss Penny released Ensley but held onto her arms. "I'm so sorry for what happened to your family." Those words, spoken in her soft and caring voice threatened to open the floodgates. The sincerity in her emerald eyes, the warmth in her touch was something Ensley hadn't seen or felt in such a long time.

Despite her best efforts to stuff down her emotions —emotions that had been bottled up for so long, moisture gathered in her eyes. The hug reminded her of every maternal thing that had been missing in Ensley's life since her mother lost it after the divorce.

"Thank you." Ensley ducked her chin to her chest to hide the moisture gathering in her eyes. She coughed and turned her head to the side.

"It's lovely to meet you. I just wish it was under better circumstances." Miss Penny clucked her tongue. "I'm happy you've found a friend in Levi." She said the word, *friend*, with uncertainty. Her gaze shifted to Levi, like she was looking for confirmation she hadn't offended anyone.

Miss Penny's gaze dropped. It was then that Ensley realized Karma was standing by her side. Levi crossed the room, fisting two coffee mugs. He went straight to the table and set them down.

Ensley and Miss Penny joined him. He looked at the woman who had been his caregiver. "Would you like a cup?"

"No, thanks. I had three this morning. If I have any more I'll vibrate so hard that I'll start an earthquake."

Ensley couldn't help but smile and it helped push her heavier emotions to the side. She liked Miss Penny. The woman had enough smile lines to say she'd had a good life. Those penetrating emerald green eyes seemed capable of sizing someone up real quick. Her slight southern lilt was endearing.

Reaching into her handbag, Ensley pulled out her journal. Levi had taken the seat next to her while Miss Penny sat at the head of the table. Ensley ran her finger along the elastic band before sliding it off and turning to the page with yesterday's date.

Next, she pulled out a pen, clicked it, and then set it down beside the journal. She took a sip of coffee and let Levi take the lead.

"Miss Penny, you're aware of Ensley's situation." Again, those emerald eyes landed on Ensley.

"I am." She reached across the table and patted Ensley's hand.

"Do you know whatever happened to Oaklynn? Does she still live in Cattle Cove?" he asked.

"Yes. She's still here," Miss Penny stated, shaking her head. "But she never recovered."

11

"What can you tell us about Greyson's and Oaklynn's families?" Levi figured the families were the best place to start. And then he could move onto those Ensley viewed as suspects.

"I can start by saying Greyson's parents were last said to be living in Austin. As you may know, he was an only child and his parents divorced in the year following his death. His mother ended up at the capital where she went to work for a politician. I hear she's one serious campaigner." Miss Penny tapped her finger on the wood table.

"Greyson's father relocated his boat repair business to Austin. Last I heard he lived somewhere near Lake Travis, I believe."

"They divorced but moved to the same city?" Levi asked as Ensley jotted down notes in her journal.

Miss Penny was rocking her head. "That's right. Both of their families were originally from the Austin area. There was a time when you couldn't live in Austin without running into each other but there's been such an influx of people moving there those days are long gone."

Levi knew how populated Austin had become. There was no end to rush hour in or around the city anymore. The Loop helped a great deal to alleviate traffic but that meant going around the city.

"What about Oaklynn? Whatever happened to her?" Ensley clicked her pen a few times before setting it on top of her journal.

Although Levi hadn't thought too much about having a family of his own, he couldn't fathom the unfairness of losing a child.

"Her parents are still married, and they still own that small farm where they're raising goats and selling goat cheese. They've done pretty well for themselves financially, but they stick to themselves ever since the incident. I can't remember the last time I saw Oaklynn. I expected her to go off to college like so many her age did when the time came, but she didn't. She stayed put to work the family business."

"Don't they have a little shop?" Levi asked.

"They do. Most of their sales are because they got picked up by a couple of big grocery chains. At least, they were. I haven't kept up with them too much in recent years. They used to be involved in our festivals and holiday celebrations. Not after..." Miss Penny's gaze flipped over Ensley and then back to Levi. "The woods."

"Do you remember about when you last saw Oaklynn?" Ensley asked.

"It's been a long time. Her father went a little berserk after what happened. He became so overprotective that he pulled her out of school and her mother homeschooled her. Folks chewed on that decision a lot. They didn't think it was good for her to be so isolated after her two best friends..." Miss Penny's gaze dropped to the table where she drew circles with her index finger. It was something she did when she talked about anything that could be painful.

Levi remembered the first time he'd noticed her habit. His youngest brother, A.J., had been due to start kindergarten and their mother had been planning a party for him. She was going to do it up, balloons and all. A freak storm produced a flash flood that swept her vehicle off the bridge. She never made it to the store.

"No one in town felt like they had the right to tell anyone else how to bring up their children, let alone after what that family had been through," Miss Penny continued. "You know who I never really liked?" She wagged her finger. "Oaklynn's older brother, Ren. I never did like that boy."

"Someone had to know the three of them were out there." Levi looked to Ensley. "Is it possible they told someone? Him?"

"Anything is possible, but I doubt it. All three of them stood to be in a lot of trouble for pulling a stunt like that. I doubt any of them wanted to get caught and telling anyone would be risky."

"Maybe we could start a list of anyone who might have figured it out." Levi nodded toward Ensley's journal.

She picked up her pen and clicked it. She wrote the word, *Names*.

Underneath it, she started a list. Ren, was first.

"There was always something a little bit different about him," she agreed. "He was a couple of years younger than me in school. That would make him... what?...about three years older than my brother. Since Cooper was twelve about to turn thirteen when this happened, that would put Ren at about fifteen or maybe sixteen."

She circled Ren's name.

"Were there any marks on Oaklynn when she came out of the woods?" Levi already knew two of the kids' throats had cuts.

Ensley shook her head. "Not one cut, despite my brother's and Greyson's condition."

"If Ren was fifteen, that might be a different story than if he was sixteen and had a license." Levi watched as Ensley wrote a dash next to Ren's name along with the numbers, fifteen and sixteen.

"You know who else always rubbed me the wrong

way aside from Ren? It was the mayor's son," Miss Penny continued.

"Harlow Beckwith's kid?" Levi asked.

"Yes. They called him Becks, I believe. It's been so long I don't remember his first name," she said.

"Garth was his first name. Garth Beckwith, but, yes, everyone called him Becks," Levi clarified.

"He was in my class. Didn't he get sent to military school?" Ensley asked.

Miss Penny was nodding her head. "He got sent off somewhere. The mayor said it was military school, but I also heard that he was sent to a halfway house. I never was really sure what happened to him."

Ensley wrote down that name.

"What about Oaklynn's father?" Levi asked. "You said he went a little crazy. Understandably so, but in Greyson's parents' case they divorced and moved off in different directions—"

"I read about that," Ensley stated. "That the divorce rate was through the roof for couples who lost a child. I was surprised my father and stepmom stayed together. I guess adoption was their way to put the past behind them and try to move on."

There was so much sadness in her voice when she talked about her parents that it hit Levi in a place he'd tried to protect. With Ensley, the attraction was strong and the walls were coming down. He reminded himself that no matter how strong the pull was to her —and it was strong—his life was here in Cattle Cove and hers was in Tennessee. She'd been clear on the fact that she couldn't wait to get out of town, and he'd spent the better part of five years of military service with one thought on his mind, *get home.*

Rather than fight the urge, he reached over and covered her hand with his. She tensed with contact and he wondered if she felt that same jolt of electricity he did. Part of him hoped so.

Instead of recoiling as he'd feared, she relaxed her hand and linked their fingers.

Miss Penny's gaze shot to their hands and then she smiled the smallest of smiles before refocusing.

"Do you know him and his wife?" Levi asked.

"We didn't run in the same circles. You know what it's like in ranching life. You see a lot of a few people— the people who impact your daily life and who you work beside. They ran that small farm and kept to themselves. After the woods, they shut down most social contact. In the beginning folks gave them plenty of space, figuring they needed time to heal. Everyone grieves differently and we all figured that was their way. Then, it seemed to drag on for months. Before we knew it, years passed and people got busy with their own lives. Oh, you'd still hear whispers every now and again about the tragedy that happened and that poor girl who survived." Miss Penny shrugged. "I guess it just got real easy to let them be."

"And there was no word from them at all?" Levi asked.

"There was some talk a while back that Mr. Stock was up to something. I don't know that anything ever came of it. You know how small towns can be. People get bored."

"There's nothing to watch on TV," he continued for her.

She was nodding her head. "People gather over at Maybelle Barnes' Sweeties Candy Bar or Alfred's DOUGH, the pizza place, and sometimes rumors get started. Everyone thought Mr. Stock was up to something but almost losing his daughter seemed to have put him on the straight and narrow again."

"What kind of talk?" Levi asked. "Like he was shorting suppliers or hitting his wife?"

Ensley withdrew her hand and then picked up the pen. She clicked it a couple of times before making a note about Mr. Stock. Then, she drew a line and wrote, *suspicious behavior*.

"I don't know if he was a violent man. His wife kept to herself unless she was out with him. They seemed happy enough on the outside but then you hear about statistics like one in four women are being abused in marriages and it makes you wonder. Mrs. Stock only went out with her husband and I know he was strict on the kids."

Apparently, Levi could write a book about what he didn't know about Cattle Cove's town folks. "What do you know about Andy Whitfield?"

"The tow truck owner? I know he's gotten people

out of a jam more than once. Why?" It seemed to dawn on her and she started rocking her head. "Right. He's Lowell Whitfield's nephew. I get it now."

"We tried talking to Andy. Didn't get a very good reaction from him," Levi said.

"That's interesting. I really didn't know Lowell Whitfield very well. It's a shame what's being written in the news about the cases. Shame on him if he covered for his friends and lied about so-called accidental deaths that were murder. I read about Nancy Sidling's death now being looked at as a homicide from seven years ago." Miss Penny pressed her hand to her chest over her heart. "It's just awful."

"Were Sheriff Skinner and Lowell Whitfield close?" Levi asked.

"Tighter than peas in a pod. And they were friends with the mayor. The three of them were poker buddies along with Judge Cox," she stated.

"That's convenient," Levi stated. "And would make getting a search warrant against any one of them tricky."

"It's always bothered me how Sheriff Skinner tried to sell what had happened to your brother and his friend."

"Andy Whitfield's son, we believe, damaged my car that was stranded on the side of the road possibly because someone tampered with it while I was in the meadow," Ensley said. "He refused to send a tow truck when he found out it was for me."

"Well, that does seem really suspicious, now doesn't it?" Miss Penny seemed incensed. "Has the new sheriff been notified?"

"She has," Ensley stated.

"What do you think about her?" Miss Penny asked Levi.

"I was about to ask you the same thing."

"I've always liked the Justice family. I've never had a bad run-in with any of them. I've never heard anything but good things. Did you say she was taking another look at the case?" Miss Penny asked Ensley.

She nodded.

"Maybe you'll get traction with a fresh set of eyes on the case. I've always believed that once someone gets locked onto an idea that's all they ever see. They lose all objectivity. Even if Skinner was trying to handle the case like a professional, and I'm not saying he was, he was so determined to blame the kids for what happened that he might've missed crucial evidence."

"He was very busy proving his theory instead of following the evidence," Ensley agreed. She blew out a frustrated-sounding breath. "All the new sheriff really has to go on are the photos from the crime scene since it happened so long ago. Obviously, the original crime scene has been trampled on dozens of times, if not more."

"The site became popular for a while on Halloween. Kids would dare each other to go into the meadow alone for a few years after. The community had to set up a watch after Randy Lobe's boy came face to face with a hungry black bear," Miss Penny said.

People could be morbid and especially teenagers.

Ensley's face screwed up like she'd been slapped. "From everything I read, DNA technology has improved over the years. If there was any DNA on the tent or backpack, it might be reasonable to think prints could be lifted. If someone besides the three of them touched either, we'd know who our killer was."

"There was a knife involved. Who wears a hunting-style knife on his hip?" Levi asked.

Miss Penny's face twisted. "Just about every male I know in the county."

True. When he really thought about it, almost everyone he knew had some kind of knife clipped to his belt. In these parts, it was handy to keep some kind of blade on the ready.

On second thought, that might not be much help.

"Okay, so that also tells me plenty of people would have a knife on them at all times." Ensley wrote the word down. "If a person accidentally stumbled onto the group, that person might already have a weapon on them."

"That would rule out premeditated murder," Levi agreed. And yet, something wasn't sitting right. "You know what? I feel like the kids had to know who their attacker was. Reason being, there were three of them, two of whom might have been young but were also fit and athletic, plus a girl who was capable of screaming her head off for help."

"No one would've heard them in the meadow. It's too far off the road," Ensley reasoned.

"What about the escaped prisoner theory. Are you certain the killer is from Cattle Cove?" he asked.

"I researched escapees from Huntsville within the timeframe of the murders. There was one name, Desi Alessandro." Ensley turned back the pages of her journal to the entry with the name.

"Were you able to rule him out?" Levi asked.

"Not exactly. But there's no way to interview him now," she stated.

"Why not?"

"Because he's dead."

12

D espite herself, Ensley remembered feeling that burst of hope that had been immediately shot down. "Desi Alessandro was killed in prison after he was returned to Huntsville a year after he escaped. I visited the prison and asked to speak to guards who said he bragged about hurting kids. Word got out and he was found strangled in his bed two days after he'd been locked up."

"Did he identify the kids?"

"No, but he was found in San Antonio and it's believed he was abusing his girlfriend's children. They were five and seven years old." Ensley picked up the pen and clicked it a couple of times—a nervous habit.

"In my mind, the killer knew the kids and he knew the area," Levi said. She needed a minute to unpack those words. It was unimaginable to think anyone could brutally kill another person. The thought it might have been someone who walked the streets of Cattle Cove or possibly the same halls at school struck her.

A very large part of Ensley needed the killer to be a blank, faceless person and not someone she might've spoken to face-to-face.

Miss Penny's cell phone buzzed. She glanced around and then fished it out of her apron pocket. The sound echoed, and Ensley realized Levi's cell was going off at the same time. An ominous feeling settled over her as she watched the two of them exchange a glance before grabbing their cells.

Levi checked the screen and immediately answered. He greeted his brother and went quiet.

"What happened?" He studied a spot on the wood table. "How?"

Ensley stared at her notebook, feeling like this was a very personal moment for Levi. Considering Miss Penny's questions were similar, Ensley figured something big was going down in their family.

Levi's gaze shifted to Karma. "I'm coming to the hospital."

Those weren't the words Ensley wanted to hear. Based on his tone, something grave had gone down.

Levi ended his call moments before Miss Penny. Her face was sheet-white and she looked shocked and a little dismayed.

"It's my father. There was an accident while he was out with his brother. I don't know all the details yet, and neither does my brother Ryan. All we know is that our father has been transported to the hospital and my Uncle Donny is with him. He had to be sedated." Levi's gaze bounced from Karma to Ensley. "I need to go but—"

"Don't worry about us. I think he'll stay with me and it'll give me a chance to clear my head. I've been thinking about the case too much and I'm getting a headache. I wouldn't mind lying down, if the offer to stay in the guest room is still on the table."

He looked to Miss Penny and said, "I can give you a ride."

"I'd like that. I'll just grab my purse and we'll be off. Okay?" She rocked her head and seemed to be gathering herself when she took in a deep breath. Her tone of voice said she was anything but that last word.

Levi fished his keys out of his pocket and glanced around the table like he was checking to see if he was missing anything. Once again, his gaze landed on Karma and a hint of desperation passed behind his eyes.

"We'll be fine." Ensley had noticed Karma was settled in between her and Levi's feet at the table. Sticking around the ranch for a few hours wouldn't hurt her investigation. She figured they were in a holding pattern at the moment anyway.

The connection between Lowell Whitfield, Sheriff Skinner and the mayor shouldn't surprise her. Throw in the judge and they pretty much had a lock on anything they wanted to get done or suppress. Her brother's case had been labeled a tragedy instead of a crime. Minds had been made up. She was making progress.

"Are you sure you'll be okay with him?" Levi asked.

"We'll figure it out. Go see your father and don't worry about what's going on here," she urged. "Just give me your phone number in case I need to reach you."

She fished out her cell and handed it over to Levi, who immediately added himself to her contacts. When he handed the phone back to her and their fingers touched, more of that electric current pulsed through her, sending a jolt straight to her heart.

Trying to ignore what was happening between them wasn't working, so she risked a glance into Levi's eyes. That same current held them there rooted in that spot for a few seconds. Time stopped and the world was reduced to the two of them. It was undeniable they both felt the attraction. The pull was fierce. What they decided to do about it, if anything at all, was completely up in the air.

Logically and logistically, trying to start a relationship was impossible. Her life was in Tennessee. Levi's whole world was here at the ranch. She hadn't even seen where he actually lived and despite feeling like she'd known him her entire life and the fact that being with him seemed like the most natural thing in the world, they were very different people.

Long-distance dating was a thing—not a thing she cared to dip into. Would she be willing to go there for the right person?

It was worth considering for Levi.

The moment happening between them broke with the sounds of feet shuffling into the room. Levi held onto Ensley's gaze a few seconds longer before he dropped down to talk to Karma at eye level.

"Be a good boy for Ensley," he said.

Karma's ears perked up.

Ensley realized they hadn't asked Miss Penny the one question that had been on her mind. "Hey, Miss Penny. Do you know who in town drives a black truck?"

"Yeah." She seemed to be searching her thoughts. "There are a few. The first one that comes to mind is Oaklynn's father."

Mr. Stock just moved to the top of the suspect list. A story was emerging. An overprotective father finds out his daughter lied to him. Furthermore, she was camping out overnight with two boys. Anyone who knew Oaklynn would realize nothing would happen. But a father might not see it that way, especially an overprotective one.

He could've been furious and figured out where the kids were. How? Ensley needed to think it through a little bit more. There were obvious holes. For one, how did he find out where they were going? Would Oaklynn have told the friend who was covering for her that night? It was a place to start. Granted, Celeste would have been traumatized by the event. She nearly lost her friend, and two schoolmates died that night. But, asking her a few questions seemed far less traumatic than trying to get to Oaklynn even if they could get past her family, which Ensley highly doubted.

There was another thing bugging her about Mr. Stock. Why was he so overprotective? Ensley understood him wanting to keep his daughter safe after her entire world was shattered. Oaklynn probably didn't want to leave the security of her own home after the killings. Maybe she believed the killer would come back for her. After her brother's death, Ensley had had the same fear herself. It had haunted her for years, leaving her unsettled and unable to sleep. At some point, though, the TV had to be clicked off. Ensley had to learn to sleep without the bedroom light on or with background noise. It had been important not to let her fears control her.

Wouldn't the Stock family want the same thing for their daughter? A normal life?

If Ensley had learned anything through this experience, it was that hiding from fear only gave it more power. The lesson had taken time and maturity.

Still hiding for almost a decade after the killings made the hairs on the back of Ensley's neck prick and an uneasy feeling settle over her. Oaklynn must be trapped in a mental prison.

"I'll be in touch when I know what's going on," Levi

said before standing up. She reached out to touch his arm and, like they had the idea at the exact same time, leaned in for more contact. Levi's arms looped around her waist as her hands reached around his neck. Bodies flush, heat ricocheted through her. One word came to mind...*home.*

Ensley cleared her throat and stepped back as Miss Penny entered the room.

"Ready when you are," she said.

Levi's gaze shot to Karma as he nodded.

"I'll take good care of him. Don't worry," Ensley reassured. The last thing she wanted Levi worrying about was his dog. He had enough on his mind.

Gripping her handbag so hard her knuckles were white, Miss Penny moved to the door.

"See you in a few hours." Levi squeezed her hand and then took off out the back door with Miss Penny.

Ensley looked at Karma. She bent down to his level, and he didn't budge. He watched the door with a weary look in his eyes.

"How about some fresh water?" She glanced around, looking for a bowl on the floor. When she found none, she popped to her feet and walked to the wall of cabinets. It took a minute, but she located a bowl that could be used for water.

After filling it, she located a dishtowel and set up his drink by the back door. Karma made his way over to her and nearly drained the small bowl. Ensley would take the win. She felt satisfied that she was able to do something for Karma.

Her stomach picked that moment to growl, reminding her she hadn't eaten since a light breakfast. She moved to the fridge and found a container full of leftovers. From the looks and smell, the leftovers were enchiladas. She located a plate and spooned out a portion before heating the meal in the microwave.

After returning the container to the fridge, she located utensils and poured a glass of water. Even though she was hungry, she didn't think she'd be able to eat. Much to her surprise, she cleared her plate in a matter of minutes. She pushed the plate aside and put the fork on top before staring at the opened page in her journal.

She clicked the pen a couple of times and then wrote two words, *someone familiar.*

Levi's assumption rang true to her, ruling out a random hiker, mental patient or prison escapee. Oaklynn's father was familiar. Everyone knew the mayor's son.

She retraced Garth's name, wondering if her brother had known him. Would he have trusted him?

When she really thought about it, the whole sneaking out thing wasn't like Cooper at all. Greyson was a good kid. She doubted the idea had come from him. Oaklynn seemed like the type to go along with her friends rather than be the ringleader. She was soft-spoken and a rule follower.

Had a third party influenced the kids or planted the seed?

All this would've been much easier if her father or stepmom had allowed Ensley access to her brother's cell phone. They'd tossed his phone along with most of his childhood belongings after they were returned from Skinner. She'd sneaked into his room and swiped his Captain America figurine. It had been his favorite toy and there was no way she could let go of it, knowing full well that if her parents caught her with it, they would've freaked.

After Cooper's death, it was like Ensley walked on eggshells around them. She still did, if she was being honest. Cooper had been the thread that had tethered her to the blended family. He'd been her little buddy and the only reason she felt like a Cartier.

Her head was splitting thinking about the case. She pulled out the photo of her brother and couldn't help but smile. This was the most progress she'd made in a decade. She had help for the first time. Support. She had Levi.

She couldn't help but think Cooper would've like the oldest McGannon. He had those rugged good looks that Cooper had wanted from the moment he'd discovered girls. Magnetic charm practically oozed off him even though he'd laugh if he heard himself described that way. There was nothing pretentious about the man. He was all strong and outdoorsy. But Cooper would've liked his sense of humor the best. She hadn't seen nearly enough of it since returning to Cattle Cove. But hints of it were there in the spark in his eyes.

Levi was smart, kind, and athletic. He had the most generous heart and, clearly, loved animals. Yeah, Cooper would've loved him all right.

Ensley tucked the photo in the journal before refilling her glass of water and then heading back into the guest room, Karma at her side.

Her suitcase was still there, opened. She toed off her shoes and tucked them under the chaise, happy that Karma had followed her to the room. He stopped at the door, turned around a couple of times and then curled into a ball, as if he felt safe here.

Taking a page out of Karma's book, she curled up on top of the covers. Her mind normally picked this moment to spin out. Overthinking had always been a problem for Ensley. It was part of the reason for her lack of sleep. Her thoughts would churn over and over in her head like a jogger on a hot track. Not this time. Not at the ranch.

Maybe it was the comfort of having security at the front gate or the fact that a well-trained military dog slept a few feet away, but she went down hard after closing her eyes.

13

By the time Ensley opened her eyes again, it was dark outside.

The mattress dipped under Levi's weight as he sat down next to her. He leaned forward and rested his elbows on his knees, clasping his hands together. Head bowed, he wore the most solemn expression.

Her heart clenched as she feared the worst.

"What happened?" She sat up.

He didn't answer.

Ensley pushed the pillow up and leaned against it. "How long was I out?"

"I got home a couple of hours ago to check on you and Karma. You looked peaceful so I let you sleep."

Save for the last twenty-four hours, she normally fell into the category of insomniac. After Cooper's death, she felt like she didn't sleep for months. After that, she had recurring nightmares. She had an unrealistic fear that whoever had killed Cooper would come after her next. Any unexpected noise made her jump. The killings might have robbed the town of its innocence, but they had stolen Ensley's childhood. Her best little buddy was taken from her and the only person in the world she'd truly felt connected to as family. The kid she'd helped get through fifth grade math and learning to write his first essay was gone. Death took away the best friend she would never know as an adult, because she was certain her and Cooper would have always remained close.

The two had formed an unbreakable bond when they were younger. But she didn't want to think about that right now. In this moment, she was more concerned with what was going on with Levi's father.

"What did the doctor say?" she asked.

"There's swelling to his brain and he's in a medically-induced coma."

"Oh, Levi. I'm so sorry. Did you say your uncle was with him? Is he okay?"

Levi issued a loaded sigh and she sensed the two weren't on good terms.

"Uncle Donny is fine. Says he doesn't know what happened. He says that one minute my dad was next to him and the next he wasn't. They were in the equipment room together and my dad was working on a tractor. Uncle Donny went to get something and came back to find my dad collapsed on the cement."

"I'm so sorry." She paused until he looked up at her and nodded. "Do you need to go back to the hospital?"

"Not right now. My family is working on a rotating schedule to make sure someone is there for Dad at all times. There's a lot of us and it was easy to see that we were overwhelming the lobby. Besides, work still needs to be done around the ranch and our father wouldn't have it any other way."

"I said it already, but I couldn't be sorrier for what you and your family are going through." Ensley reached out to touch Levi's arm to offer comfort, and a jolt of electricity ran up her fingers from contact. She tugged him toward her.

And when he looked at her, the mood in the room changed. She felt her pulse pound at the base of her throat and felt his race as she circled her fingers around his wrist.

His tongue darted across his lips as she pulled him closer. Ensley leaned into him. A moment of hesitation passed behind his eyes before their lips grazed. But when they touched, it was like lightning striking. Fire shot through her veins and every nerve ending seemed to wake at that exact moment. Her body cried out for more as she teased his tongue inside her mouth.

He tasted like dark roast coffee, her new favorite flavor.

Ensley brought her hands up to rest on Levi's shoulders, but her fingertips dug in instead. He brought his hands up to cup her face. He positioned her mouth for better access and drove his tongue into her mouth.

She'd never experienced so much passion and so much promise in one kiss in her entire life, and she found herself fleetingly sad to admit that to herself. She could see now that she'd shied away from anyone who had the slightest ability to make her feel anywhere close to this. She'd gone down the safe road dating and had kept her running shoes on hand in case the relationship heated up.

But right now, all she could do was surrender to the wave of emotion coursing through her, awakening parts of her she never knew existed.

In a matter of minutes, her breath was robbed. She dug her fingers into Levi's muscled shoulders even more to ground herself. Before she could debate her actions, she'd scooted on top of his lap, facing him, with her legs on either side of his thighs.

Their tongues twined and her body ached to get lost in him.

He pulled back first and she could hear his ragged breathing. He pressed his forehead to hers like he needed a minute to collect his thoughts.

Still breathless from the kiss, still aching for more, it took a second for Ensley to process the fact he'd done the right thing. Yes, she could get lost in the moment with him and she had no doubt sex with Levi would blow her mind.

But then what?

A few awkward exchanges while he helped her on the case? Or, worse, he dropped out because their feelings got in the way? She couldn't imagine Levi McGannon doing anything less than the honorable thing—and that would be to see this through to the end. How horrible would it feel to know he was helping her out of obligation? And a man with his morals would never leave her stranded. Granted, a guy as smokin' hot in every way as Levi could leave a string of women in his wake. He could be a real love 'em and leave 'em jerk who left a trail of broken hearts. But that wasn't his nature. He'd dated one girl at a time in high school and never seemed to need to have someone hanging off his arm when he wasn't in a relationship. His self-confidence was most likely a very large part of what had drawn her to him all those years ago in the first place. And it was sexier than all get-out now.

There was nothing hot about a guy who couldn't spend five minutes outside of a relationship without needing to fill a void.

When it came to Levi, he had his own orbit. She'd seen a glimpse of it when she was young and their age gap mattered. He hadn't given her a second look back then, and rightfully so.

But her feelings toward him now shocked her out of her comfort zone. Despite all the confused thoughts running around in her head—thoughts that made her want to stick around and explore the possibilities between them—she realized she'd been setting her standards for relationships too low. Comfortable and non-threatening were probably not the best words to describe a budding relationship, and yet those two came to mind when she attempted to describe her past.

If nothing else, Levi McGannon had shown her what it was like to be with someone who could give it all to her...passion, excitement and a soul-deep love.

"Is this a mistake?" Levi's breath came out in rasps and a sensual shiver spread over her when he spoke.

"I want this as much as you do. Maybe more." Ensley brought her hands up to his face, tracing the curve of his powerful jawline. She traced a line up to his ears and let her fingers get lost in his thick dark mane. Looking into those eyes stirred her heart and released a dozen butterflies in her stomach.

"If things went any further between us, it would be impossible to walk away unscathed," he said.

"There's no question that I have feelings for you, Levi. There's no question in my mind that if we had sex it would be mind-blowing."

A small smile tugged at the corners of those perfect lips and his face broke into a cocky little grin. "Did you say *mind-blowing*?"

She playfully slapped at his arm and was met with rock-hard muscle.

"Try not to get all egotistical." She locked gazes with him, a deadly mistake as pure primal need stared back at her.

"If we go down that road, and I'm not saying we shouldn't, it's going to be a game-changer for me." He paused for a second. "I can't make it work in my head..."

He stopped right there.

"Go on."

"Other than the obvious fact that we don't live in the same city or want the same things in life?"

"I thought about that already." So why did her chest deflate?

"Here's the thing, Ensley. Whatever *this* is that's going on between us is the most real thing I've felt in a very long time. I've been in enough relationships and been alive long enough to know this is different. This has the potential to be something very real. Part of me says to go down that path with you, see where it takes us. And I think I could do that. But can you?"

"What does that mean?"

"Can you let someone in? And I mean all the way in? Or, more specifically, can you let *me* in?"

"Believe me when I say the answer that I want to give to that question is yes. I can honestly say that I've never been with anyone who makes me feel the way you do. No one has even come close. There's no question in my mind that whatever is happening between us is special."

He nodded and some of the knot that had formed in her stomach loosened.

"If I could go there with anyone...it would be you.

Hands down." She stopped right there because she didn't want to say the words that could hurt both of them. While they were unspoken, it felt like there was a possibility, a chance, that everything could just magically work out between them.

"Geography is a problem," she added. They both knew it was more like an excuse, but it was very real that his life was on the ranch and hers was in Tennessee. "Being back here...there are just so many memories."

Too many?

He nodded.

"Though it feels different when I'm with you." She had no idea how or why or what that meant. She also had no idea if that explanation helped him at all. All she knew for certain was the way he patiently listened to her grounded her, tethering her to reality again. And a good reality this time. One she very much wanted to spend more time in.

The problem between them was still the same. Could she go there enough to make it worth the risk for him?

Levi leaned in and pressed a long, slow kiss to her lips. Heat simmered below the surface and came off him in waves as their soft lips melded into one.

This time, when he pulled back, a wall came up between them. Levi moved to the chaise lounge and sat down. He leaned his elbows on top of his knees and clasped his hands together in a defensive position.

Everything inside Ensley wanted to get off that bed, walk over to him and then drop down to eye level. She wanted to make promises to him that she feared would be impossible to keep.

Despite how much her heart wanted all those things, something in her mind stopped her.

"See you in the morning." He stood up and then walked out of the room.

14

Levi had already been awake for a solid two hours by the time Ensley joined him. He got in an early morning workout and went through Karma's routine with him. Seeing her dressed in an oversized t-shirt and hair still messy from sleep felt a little too right. "Morning."

Her eyes lit up and she briefly smiled.

"I've been thinking a lot about what you said earlier," she said.

"What was that?" He knew it wasn't about their non-relationship based on her expression and the fact that she clutched the journal in her hand. As much as he wanted to go there with her emotionally, he understood why she couldn't. He didn't like it but it made sense.

Then again, what was he offering her exactly? The details were as clear as dirt water.

"I couldn't sleep last night," she stated. A selfish piece of him wished part of that had to do with how they'd left things last night and less about the case.

He knew that was asking too much. Hell, he didn't even know if he was in a position to offer anything of himself to her. He wasn't kidding when he'd told her that instinct said whatever was developing between them was special. A relationship with Ensley would be a game-changer and there was no way he could cope with just having one night with her. That realization really plastered a smile on his face. He couldn't remember the last time he'd turned down the possibility of mind-numbing, mind-blowing sex with an attractive and intelligent woman who was interested in exactly the same thing he wanted—sex with no emotional strings attached—and nothing more.

Levi chalked the changes in him up to the foreign feelings he had with Ensley, and his smile faded as he reminded himself that he needed to get over it. She'd been pretty clear with where they stood last night, and he should thank her for being direct instead of licking his bruised ego. "What did I say?"

"Someone familiar." She started toward the coffee machine. He put his hand up to stop her.

"I got this." He made quick work of the machine and brought over a fresh mug. One for her and then one for him. He took a seat beside her at the table. Their outer thighs touched and more of that inconvenient attraction surged. He called on more of his own willpower to tamp down his reaction to her—willpower that had never seemed in short supply until her.

"Is there anyone in particular on your mind this morning?"

"My mind just keeps going back to Oaklynn's father. I mean, the killer had to be someone familiar because there were two of them, three if you count Oaklynn, and only one of him. It would take someone pretty savvy to be able to trick all three of them."

"Wouldn't Oaklynn know who her own father is?"

"That's not the right question. You saw how protective Boyd was of his father. It reminded me how tightknit families are in Cattle Cove. Maybe she's protecting her father. Maybe she thinks she doesn't have a choice. Think about it; who keeps their kid home and never lets them go back to school? My parents tried everything to get back to a 'normal' life."

"I keep going back to motive. What motive would her father have of killing two young boys? Granted, they were out with his daughter in the woods. But your brother and his friend weren't the kind of kids who would lure a girl out to a remote place and take advantage of her. That is literally the only reason I could think of that might make her father go a little crazy and possibly, in the heat of the moment, kill them. But this is Cooper and Greyson we are talking about. They were good kids. They didn't seem to step out of line outside of being normal preteen kids. It's hard to

believe anyone would have it out for them and especially one of their best friend's father." Levi saw
Ensley's shoulders sag more and more. He didn't want
to be the bearer of bad news, but it just logically didn't
fit together. If Mr. Stock was the killer, he and Ensley
were missing something.

"All good points. But I think there's something
there. Something that we're missing." Ensley's cell
phone buzzed. She checked the screen and frowned.

"Who is it?" Levi asked as he took a sip of coffee.

She showed him the screen. The number looked
familiar, but he couldn't place it.

"I gave the sheriff my phone number yesterday
when I was giving her my statement." Ensley took the
call and put the phone to her ear. She immediately
locked gazes with him and nodded. "Do you mind if I
put you on speaker? I have Levi here with me."

The sheriff must not have objected because Ensley
set the phone in between them and hit the button for
the speaker.

"I've had a chance to review the file and look at the
case from the perspective of a fresh pair of eyes on the
evidence," the sheriff began after greeting Levi.

"I thought the file was missing other than a few
pictures," Ensley quickly interjected.

"It was right where it was supposed to be when I
looked for it," the sheriff said.

Ensley issued a sharp sigh. "So, we were lied to."

"It seems so," the sheriff confirmed.

"Does that mean you found something?" Levi asked the sheriff.

"There's something that's bothering me from the crime scene photos. Keep in mind that I'm at a disadvantage not having been there in person. However, there was a backpack on the scene and I'm hoping you can tell me who it belongs to."

"What kind and color?" Ensley perked up.

"It was a black and royal blue camouflage."

"That was Cooper's," she said.

"Are you certain?"

"Yes. He loved that thing. He got it as a present before going into middle school and kept it through what would've been his third year. He planned to take it all the way through high school."

"Was it a popular brand?" Justice asked.

"No. Greyson was obsessed with hockey and had a green backpack from the Dallas team. Oaklynn's was purple and her grandmother had stitched a horse on it for her. Oaklynn had had it since she was in elementary school but wouldn't let go of it because her grandmother passed away the summer before middle school. It was important to her and she never went anywhere without it. I remember that thing explicitly because I can't count the number of times I had to ask her to move it off the kitchen counter so I could make dinner. It grossed me out thinking of all the bathroom floors she'd probably set it on while using the facilities." Ensley paused before asking,

"Why? What do backpacks have to do with anything?"

"The backpack was tossed into a tree. I have a theory about it that I hope will lead us to answers." The sheriff hadn't used the words, *to the killer*.

"What's your theory?" Levi asked. "And how can a backpack in a tree lead you to where you want to go?"

"Someone might have picked up the backpack and threw it in the tree. My theory is that the person did it to mark the spot of the killings." Those last couple of words had Ensley sitting ramrod straight.

"Why would they do that?" she asked.

"So they could find the spot again. Relive it. Sometimes it's so they can know when searchers are getting close so they can lead them away from the bodies or enjoy watching them be found."

It made sense that if someone had gone to the trouble to mark the scene, they might still monitor the area if they live here.

The sheriff continued, "It's possible a killer struck the boys and Oaklynn got away. I've read the files and the reports from the psychiatrist she spoke to. Oaklynn remembers hearing voices and loud shouting. She said it sounded like they came from inside a tunnel. It's possible her mind blocked out many of the details due to shock. She said she couldn't be certain if the boys were shouting at each other or someone else."

"Levi mentioned something yesterday that has been sticking in my mind," Ensley began. "He thinks my brother and Greyson were killed by someone familiar to them."

"That wouldn't conflict with my theory. Although, to be fair, a murder weapon was never found. I did go back to the evidence room and was able to find the backpack still in a Ziploc. I'm packing it up and sending it to Quantico for analysis. DNA technology has come a long way in the past ten years. The texture of the material isn't great for lifting prints, so I'm not making any promises, but my hope is that we can get at least a partial."

"How long will that take?" she asked.

"Investigations aren't like what you see on TV. It can take weeks or even months depending on how backed up they are at Quantico. I'll follow up and stay on it but it's not uncommon for this to move slowly with their backlog."

Ensley blew out a frustrated sigh. She picked up the journal and pulled out the picture of her brother.

"I'm sorry I don't have a definitive answer. But this is a direction that I feel good about. This is progress and these things take time." The sheriff was over-explaining, no doubt not wanting to get Ensley's hopes up but at the same time wanting her to know work was being done.

"I appreciate everything you're doing to find my brother's killer."

"You're welcome. But we're just getting started here."

"Is it possible at all to see Oaklynn?" Ensley asked.

"That's a little difficult right now for obvious reasons. Not the least of which is that her father fiercely protects her," the sheriff said.

"I understand. But I wonder what would happen if she saw me again. And I also wonder if she's at home because she wants to be. She's an adult now. She could come and go as she liked."

"I've been into the store to buy goat cheese and she shies away from working the counter, but I haven't seen any signs that she's being held against her will."

A look passed behind Ensley's eyes and Levi knew exactly what she was thinking.

"One other thing. Boyd Whitfield confessed to taking his father's truck without his knowledge and vandalizing your car," Sheriff Justice said.

"Why would he do that?" Ensley's question was the first that popped into Levi's mind.

"Confess or commit the crime?"

"I guess my first questions are why would he care if I'm in town and how did he know who the car belonged to?"

"He claims that he overheard his father refusing the call. Said he didn't know who you were—"

Ensley issued a sharp sigh.

"I never said I believed him," the sheriff quickly added, and the comment seemed to give Ensley a boost of confidence in the sheriff's ability to read people.

"The coincidence sounds sketchy if you ask me," Ensley said.

"Right," Justice agreed.

"It also gets his father off the hook." Ensley tapped her finger on the wood table. She picked up the pen and clicked it a few times.

"I do find it interesting that he would come forward voluntarily." Based on the sheriff's tone, she wasn't buying any of this.

"Did he give a reason?" Ensley asked.

"Claimed it was a harmless prank. Says that as soon as he learned it was in front of the 'haunted' site he wanted to play a joke." The sheriff's emphasis on the word, *haunted*, gave the impression she wasn't thrilled with repeating the word.

Ensley clicked the pen a couple more times. Her grip on it caused her knuckles to go white. Levi sat as he watched her go through all of this, *suffer* through all of this. He wished there was something he could do to take away the pain in her eyes and in her heart. The frustration he'd felt when Karma first came to the ranch and Levi had no idea how to help the dog resurfaced.

Levi clenched and released his fists a couple of times to try to ease some of his tension. It was also a good way to keep his hands busy because they wanted to reach out to Ensley.

A moment of silence passed before the sheriff spoke again. "I'll be in touch if I have any other questions. Sit tight for me. Just because we're waiting on this particular piece of evidence to come back doesn't mean I won't be doing everything in my power to go about finding the truth another way."

The sheriff's reassurance seemed to strike a chord with Ensley. She thanked Sheriff Justice again. After ending the call, Ensley focused on Levi. He could read her mind and couldn't help but wonder if visiting Oaklynn was a good idea. His heart went out to the young woman. She'd survived losing her best friends at a critical age. The killings seemed to make her afraid of her own shadow. Levi didn't want to add to Oaklynn's pain. But at the same time, if her family ran a store anyone should be able to stop by. He looked up at Ensley and asked, "Are you thinking about goat cheese?"

Ensley tucked the picture of her brother inside her journal. Her movements were fluid, rehearsed. She moved with the kind of ease that said she'd been performing this same motion for a long time. She carefully closed the elastic band around the journal to secure the pages and then stood up. "I sure am."

Levi glanced down at Karma. His skills were about to be put to the test. He hoped Karma was ready to interact with more people. There was no way he was leaving his dog to fend for himself.

Tricky didn't begin to describe the situation. Common sense said Levi should ask one of his brothers to step in to help Ensley. Logic wasn't ruling his decisions at the moment. He would worry about unpacking that later. Right now, he had an errand to run.

Just as they got ready to leave, Miss Penny walked in through the back door. She'd been at his father's side all night and looked like she was staying awake on a thread. The memory of seeing his father in a hospital bed slammed into Levi like a rogue wave. He issued a sharp breath.

"How is he?" Levi asked.

"The good news is that he's not worse. The bad news is that he's not better. Although, the doctor seemed to think that was positive." She put her hand on the counter like it was the only thing holding her upright. "The doctor also says that with the kind of blow he took to the head we're possibly in for a long road. They never know how someone's body or brain is going to respond. For now, he's breathing through a tube and he's being monitored closely. I'm sorry I don't have better news."

Miss Penny's easy smile had been replaced by deep worry lines. She tried to force cheer in her voice but it was too hoarse to pull it off. She sounded like she needed to go straight to bed.

"Thank you for the update." Levi wasn't due to be at the hospital until later that night but he appreciated every little update that Miss Penny and his brothers had been sending.

Miss Penny looked to Ensley. "How are you holding up?"

Ensley inclined her head quietly. "I'm hanging in there."

"Sometimes that's the best we can hope for." The look of solidarity that passed between the two women caused Levi's chest to squeeze. His heart warmed at the thought of two people he cared about getting along. The notion was foreign because he'd never cared what other people thought about who he dated, and he and Ensley weren't exactly a couple, no matter how much his heart wanted to argue different. She was special to him. The pull toward her was stronger than anything he'd experienced before. And he knew in his heart she was different than anyone else he'd ever spent time with. Their circumstances couldn't be more opposite. He could never imagine leaving the land that was part of his soul any more than Ensley could see her life back here in Cattle Cove. So, yeah, complicated didn't begin to describe their situation.

Levi shook it off and checked the fridge. "There are a few leftovers in here. Do you want me to heat something up for you before we head out?"

Miss Penny was already shaking her head before he finished his sentence. "Nothing for me, thanks. All I need is a toothbrush and a soft bed. I came home to grab a toothbrush and get a couple hours of sleep before heading back."

"What about Uncle Donny?" Levi didn't trust his uncle as far as he could throw him.

"He isn't saying much. He's resting and they put him on some pretty heavy medication. I wanted to warn you that he will most likely be released and back here at the big house in a couple of hours." She paused long enough to issue a sharp sigh. "For what it's worth, he's beside himself."

Levi bit his tongue. He would just bet that Uncle Donny was concerned about the free ride ending that he'd been on due to Levi's father's good heart. Though this really wasn't the time to point it out.

"What about the others? Everyone doing okay under the circumstances?" As the oldest, Levi had always felt a sense of responsibility to look out for his siblings and cousins.

Levi figured he and Ensley would be away from home for the next few hours at the very least and he was fine with not seeing Uncle Donny for a while. Levi was still trying to figure out how his uncle could've been in the exact same room and not seen or heard anything from Levi's father. Levi figured he could scratch his head all day wondering what made his Uncle Donny tick and come up with no answers. The man was the exact opposite of all five of his sons, his brother, and all of his nephews.

But he guessed every family had a Donny.

"I hope you can get some rest," Levi said to Miss

Penny. He had a feeling they were going to be in for a long ride on this one.

"I'll just get a couple hours of shut-eye, then eat something and head back over. Think you'll be staying here at the big house?" Not much got past Miss Penny, and especially not the fact that Levi didn't care much for his uncle despite never uttering the words out loud. He would never insult the man in public for fear it might hurt his cousins.

"We'll be here." Levi wanted to make it clear to Ensley that he wanted her to stick around.

Miss Penny nodded before starting across the room. She stopped mid-kitchen and then turned to face Levi, who was already at the door, Karma by his side, and his hand linked with Ensley's.

"Oh, one more thing. I was talking to Sheila's mom, Ruth, about folks in the town. Ruth is a nurse at General and she's been around for a long time. She told me that Garth never did go away to military school like we all thought."

Levi's pulse kicked up a few notches at the revelation. "Where did he go?"

"You'll never believe this. He was sent off to a halfway house. Apparently, he spent a little time at the psych ward here in the hospital. He was considered a danger to himself. A doctor at the hospital was going to commit him, but the mayor intervened and it was agreed that he would go to a halfway house nearby instead."

The muscles in Ensley's hand contracted.

"Did she say anything about the timing?" Levi was performing a mental calculation.

"According to Ruth, it would've been around the time of the murders."

Levi could feel Ensley's gaze on him before he even turned to look at her. He nodded, taking this new information into consideration with what they already knew. If Garth 'Becks' as they called him, was in a halfway house nearby, it was possible he could've had access to the meadow.

"We need to know the exact timing," Levi said low, so only Ensley could hear him. His mind already started spinning. It would be impossible to get information from halfway houses about a patient and no one at the hospital would be able to discuss a patient's file. Also, this happened ten years ago.

And yet, Levi found that bit of information deeply unsettling.

"Thank you for letting us know." There had to be some way they could look this up and verify the information. He tightened his grip on Ensley's hand and walked her out to the truck.

After tapping the key fob to unlock the doors and opening one for Karma, Levi stepped back letting the dog perform the ritual that would allow him some peace.

Becks, the mayor's son, in a halfway house two towns over around the time of the murders. *Interesting.*

"We need to stop by the sheriff's office and clue her in to this new piece of information," he said to Ensley.

"You know this possibly implies a town-wide cover up at the highest levels of leadership." Ensley's words were exactly the same ones rolling through Levi's mind as he navigated onto the main road.

15

The farm was on the west end of Cattle Cove. From the road, a large pasture and acres of rolling hills were visible. The front gate was opened, and an iron sign hung over the drive with the words, *Stock Farms.*

The place looked so serene and welcoming. There was a small gravel road leading to a parking lot that was located beside a quaint whitewashed building with hunter green shutters. STOCK was spelled out in the same color of green over the door.

Levi backed into a spot nearest the door and Ensley realized it was so they could make a quick escape.

"Do you want to stay here in the truck with Karma?" she asked. The dog was on full alert, standing on all fours on the bench seat in between them.

"I don't want you going in there alone."

"Fair point. But, it might be hard on Karma if he's

not able to 'clear' the building and you would just be right here in the truck if I dashed inside. I'm fairly certain that I'll get booted out right away if Mr. Stock sees me. I have no idea how Oaklynn's mother might react to my presence. Or Oaklynn. Part of me thinks she might not even remember me at all if she truly blocked everything out."

"You won't know until you go in there." Levi had a pretty tight grip on the steering wheel. His head was cocked to one side, a telltale sign he was rolling over ideas in his head. "How about if I put Karma on his leash and we walk the perimeter of the building while you're inside?"

"That works for me if you think that's the best idea."

"It's the best way for me to be within earshot if you need me."

"Good point. I don't exactly know what I'm walking into, and it does seem like people in town are already aware that I'm here."

"Okay. Let's do it." Levi made a move to hook the leash on Karma, who hadn't stepped down. This was a new area that he'd never been to and it was evidenced by the stress on his face. Ensley wished that he didn't have to come with them, but she couldn't imagine leaving him back at the ranch. It was difficult for him to be thrown into normal life after being highly trained for missions.

"Here goes nothing." Ensley threw her shoulder

into the truck's door as she pulled the lever. She issued a sharp sigh.

Levi and Karma were already going out the driver's side and Karma had snapped into training mode. Nose to the ground, he was making a straight line toward the nearest vehicle. She figured it would take him a minute or two to clear those before starting on the main building. She didn't want to cause him any undue worry or stress. She'd be in and out.

As she walked up to the front door and onto the small porch, her pulse kicked up a few notches. By the time she opened the wooden door with glass panels, her heart was at a full gallop.

The moment she opened the door, a bell chimed. She stepped inside the small room with the bar height counter. There was a cash register to one side. A couple of two-top tables dotted the room along with several glass-door refrigerators with Stock Farms Goat Cheese packages in various sizes.

There was an opened door a few feet behind the counter that led to the backroom.

"Someone will be right with you." The last time Ensley had heard that voice was ten years ago. It had sounded a lot younger then but was unmistakable now.

Ensley walked up to the counter. She opened her mouth to speak but her voice failed her. She cleared her throat and tried again.

"Oaklynn?" she finally croaked.

"I said that someone will be there to help you in a minute." There was a shocked quality to the voice, which gave Ensley the impression people didn't come by to ask for her.

"I'm here to see you, Oaklynn." The frog in Ensley's throat distorted her voice. "It's me. Ensley Cartier. Cooper's sister."

Ensley waited as quiet gripped the room.

"No one's here to help you right now." There was a desperate child-like quality to Oaklynn's voice now.

This seemed like the right time to round the counter and head toward the stockroom. Heart slamming against her ribs so hard it hurt, Ensley made her way to the door. Logic said Oaklynn would be twenty-two years old by now.

The room had walls of refrigerators with two wooden desks that faced each other from across the room. The one to the right was the one where Oaklynn sat. Ensley half expected to run into the twelve-year-old girl Oaklynn had been.

She'd aged, unlike Cooper.

"You're so much older now and still so beautiful," Ensley said, struggling with her own emotions.

Tears sprang to Oaklynn's eyes.

Oaklynn's skin paled and she grabbed her hair before leaning over and retching into what most likely was a trashcan. After a few productive heaves, she shouted, "Go away."

Ensley had no idea why Oaklynn had just become

so violently ill at the sight of her. Guilt? Sadness? Had she been holding in her feelings for the past ten years? Was it *that* difficult to see Cooper's sister again?

"I'm here, Oaklynn. And I'm not going anywhere until I figure out what happened that night with my brother." A quick scan of the room told Ensley the two of them were alone. She figured she might not get this moment again.

Oaklynn was shaking her head and trying to shoo Ensley away with her left hand while holding her hair back with her right. After a couple of heaves, she barked, "It's dangerous for you here. Leave here *now* and get out of town."

"I'm sorry, Oaklynn. I can't do that. I'm not going anywhere."

The young woman turned her head and shot Ensley a death glare. Oaklynn's long, kinky-blond hair and blue eyes reminded Ensley so much of the beautiful preteen she'd been. When Oaklynn's eyes locked onto Ensley's, something moved behind those baby blues.

"Whatever it is, you can tell me."

Oaklynn almost violently shook her head. "You don't understand. It's not safe for you here. Go back to wherever you've been for the last ten years. Forget about this. It won't bring him back." Her voice faltered when she spoke about Cooper.

Ensley figured this was the closest she would have in a long time. Even seeing Oaklynn reminded her so much about her brother. Ensley reached inside her bag and located the journal. She walked over to the desk as she carefully slipped off the elastic band.

She pulled out the picture of Cooper. There was so much sympathy for Oaklynn, and yet her reactions made her seem guilty or like she knew something, and that something filled Ensley's whole world.

There was no telling how long the two of them would be alone. Oaklynn had made it seem like someone was coming.

The only ammunition Ensley had was the picture of her brother. She could only pray that it might spur Oaklynn to start talking, but when the young woman glanced at the photo, she burst into tears. And she seemed even more determined not to speak.

"I just spoke to Sheriff Justice. She sent Cooper's backpack to Quantico for DNA analysis." She kept her gaze trained on Oaklynn, who refused to look at either Ensley or the picture. "The killer's prints are going to be on that backpack. It was moved. It's going to take a couple of weeks, maybe a month, but you can help me now. Either way, the killer is going to be revealed."

Oaklynn looked miserable and it nearly cracked Ensley's heart in half to be the one causing that young woman more pain. She was holding onto a secret. Protecting her father? Ensley had no idea what kind of parent Mr. Stock had been. Based on what she'd heard recently, he loved his daughter. Too much? It was possible he found out about the kids' plan and went

berserk. Ensley knew in her gut that there was a critical piece of information or evidence missing.

She was so close to getting the answer her soul
craved, to getting justice for her murdered brother.

"I don't know what you're talking about. You're
lying," Oaklynn shot back. "There was no killer. There
was me, Cooper, and Greyson. Now, they're gone and
there's nothing we can do to bring them back."

She started rocking back and forth like a child. She
covered her ears like she couldn't bear to hear
anymore.

The urge to go to her and hug her was an almost
overwhelming force. Being this close to an answer
after a decade of fear and suspicion and grief was
almost unthinkable. Taking a hard line physically hurt
Ensley but she thought it might be the only way to
help Oaklynn through the shock she was experiencing. And yet, pushing the young woman, who seemed
so much like a girl right now, was impossible. It was
obvious Oaklynn was experiencing some type of
PTSD and Ensley's heart broke as she helplessly
watched.

The living nightmare that had practically
consumed all of Ensley's adult life was so close to
getting closure and yet outside of her grasp. Ensley
hated doing this. She hated the thought of bringing
more pain to this young person.

Oaklynn knew something she wasn't sharing.

Did she know who the killer was? Had she seen

him that night? Had she been able to identify his voice but chose to hide information instead?

The only person Ensley could see doing that for would be family. What other reason would cause Oaklynn to lie to the sheriff? Or was she 'fed' a statement? Was she told what to say and how to say it?

The conspiracy theory bubbled to the surface. Had Becks been involved?

Ensley moved around the desk until she was right in front of Oaklynn, who was dry heaving. Maybe a softer tact would lead to a breakthrough. Ensley was out her league here despite having suffered her own personal hell for the past ten years.

"My brother's killer has been walking around free for ten years, Oaklynn. Whatever happened wasn't your fault. You didn't do anything wrong. My brother didn't deserve to die." She grabbed the picture off the table and put it directly in Oaklynn's field of view. The girl slammed her eyes shut harder, rocking back and forth even harder than before.

Ensley reached her arm up and grabbed onto Oaklynn's wrist, pulling her hand away from her ear as gently as she could. Her heart bled for Oaklynn, but she couldn't stop now.

"Cooper's killer should not be walking around free. He shouldn't get away with this and be allowed to hurt someone else." Ensley wasn't getting through with the hard line. She thought about how protective families were in Cattle Cove, about Andy Whitfield's son, who'd confessed to a crime he may or may not have committed to protect his flesh and blood.

Was Oaklynn covering for her father?

Taking a look at the clearly distraught young woman, Ensley realized that she should be taking a softer approach, both if she was going to get through and also because she didn't want to cause any more hurt to the girl who'd once been such a vibrant part of Cooper's life.

"I know my brother cared about you a lot. And you cared about him, too," she began. Those words caused Oaklynn to wrench even harder. "Was it your father?"

Oaklynn almost violently shook her head and quickly drew back like she'd been slapped. It wasn't the reaction Ensley hoped for because she'd been banking on the fact Oaklynn's father had been responsible. It was the only thing that made sense.

Why would Oaklynn care about the mayor's son if it had been him? Had she been threatened?

The kind of violent illness that had overcome her was such a red flag. Guilt?

Ensley held onto the photo, keeping it exactly where Oaklynn could see. "You're so much older now. Not Cooper. Not Greyson. This was it for them. They're frozen in time and will never age. We deserve answers. You can help me. I know you can. You've been quiet about this for ten years and maybe it's eating you from the inside out. It doesn't have to be like that anymore."

Tears streaked Oaklynn's face and this was the first hint that Ensley might be getting through.

"You can tell me who is responsible. You don't have to hide it anymore. You were the only one who walked out of there alive, Oaklynn. Some people think you were involved or at the very least covering up—"

A cry tore from Oaklynn's throat. "I would never hurt my best friends."

At least Oaklynn was talking now.

Ensley bent down on her knees to get to eye level in front of Oaklynn. "I'm begging you. Give my family some peace. I can't move on until I know what happened to him."

The back door slammed open and Oaklynn gasped at the same time Ensley did. She shot to her feet and tucked the picture of her brother into her journal, loosely jamming both inside her handbag.

"Daddy." There was a mix of fear and anger in Oaklynn's voice now.

Ensley spun around to the tune of a medium height, medium build man pointing a shotgun directly at her. Mr. Stock had a thick head of gray hair, a round midsection and a bulbous nose. She still recognized him but it looked like he'd aged twenty years in the past ten.

"Get off my property. Get off my land. You're trespassing."

Hands in the surrender position, palms out, so that

he could see she wasn't carrying a weapon, Ensley said, "I just came to buy some goat cheese, Mr. Stock."

She knew better than to taunt the man. There was so much anger radiating from him as it was.

"We're sold out. Like I said, get off my property. You're trespassing."

Oaklynn began trembling.

"With all due respect, Mr. Stock, I'm just stopping by a store. That doesn't exactly make me a criminal. You do sell a product and I am a customer. That's not the definition of trespassing."

"You have no business being back here." He glanced around the room, but she had the feeling that statement covered so much more ground.

She started toward the door, figuring the man wouldn't think twice about firing a shot.

"It's my fault, Daddy. I didn't hear the bell. I don't feel well." Oaklynn clutched her stomach and doubled over. "She just came back here looking for somebody to help her."

Mr. Stock angled the shotgun toward the door. "Well, now that you've found someone you best be on your way. Like I said, we don't have any more goat cheese for sale today."

The door opened. The bell jingled. Ensley heard Levi's reassuring voice trying to calm Karma.

16

P anic gripped Ensley at the thought Mr. Stock might aim the barrel of his shotgun at Karma and provoke him, so she took another couple of steps backward, towards the door.

"Everything is okay in here, Levi. I'm coming out. Mr. Stock has a shotgun pointed at me and has asked me to leave." She needed to make sure that Levi had all the facts so that he could take the appropriate precautions. One wrong move and she feared Mr. Stock might get trigger happy.

"Get out of here, Oaklynn," Mr. Stock demanded. His harsh tone sent a chill racing down Ensley's back.

Oaklynn cleared her throat and said, "It's okay, Daddy."

In a surprising move, she walked around the desk and placed her own body in between Ensley and her father's shotgun barrel.

"Do what I said, Oaklynn," her father demanded.

"Not anymore, Daddy. Put that down or I'll tell everything I know." The threat seemed to anger Mr. Stock even more. His round face reddened with anger.

"I'm coming out, Levi." She could hear a low-throaty growl from Karma and figured he was agitated because he wasn't able to secure the area. Dogs were known to pick up on fear and adrenaline and there was plenty of that going around.

She needed to get him and Levi out of there before the situation escalated. As soon as Ensley cleared the room, she heard a shotgun blast. Her gaze flew to Oaklynn, who'd jumped at the sound.

Scanning her body, Ensley was relieved that she didn't see a bullet or shotgun wound. It must've been a warning shot and, trust her, it had the intended effect. Ensley was scared. Karma bolted into action.

Nose to the floor, he was agitated being on the leash that was extended as far as it could go. There was no slack in the leash and Levi seemed to be working hard to keep Karma from gaiting into the backroom.

Everything next happened in slow motion. Oaklynn screamed for her father to stop. Ensley practically tackled the young woman from behind and then dragged her out through the front door.

Levi and Karma followed while the trained dog barked like there was no tomorrow.

"Come with us," she said to Oaklynn. "We'll find a safe place for you."

Oaklynn leaned into Ensley.

"I'll never be able to come home again," she said as she was ushered off the porch.

At the truck, Ensley stopped. "I want you to come with us. I think it's dangerous for you to be here now. But it's your choice. I can't force you to do anything you don't want to nor would I want to. So, what are you going to do? Stay here or go with us?"

Levi was urging them to get inside the vehicle. He opened the passenger door and, thankfully, Karma hopped inside.

"What will it be?" Ensley could only hope the young woman would make the right call.

Oaklynn chewed on her bottom lip until it bled and every muscle in her body tensed. She looked to be debating her next actions intensely.

"We can get help. You don't have to stay here against your will if you don't want to."

Oaklynn issued a sharp sigh before climbing into the back seat of the truck. Ensley climbed in beside her at the same time Oaklynn's father stepped onto the front porch. Ensley wrapped an arm around the shivering young lady.

Levi hit the gas. Gravel spewed underneath the tires until they gained enough traction to tear out of the parking lot.

"You're doing the right thing. I'll do everything in my power to help you," Ensley whispered to Oaklynn.

The younger woman curled into a ball, burrowing into Ensley's side.

"There's a blanket." Levi motioned toward the backseat as a shotgun blast split the air.

She located the throw blanket that had been tucked into the back of the driver's seat.

"Duck down and stay hidden." Levi slid low in his seat as he started zigzagging the truck. "Someone should get the sheriff on the line."

Ensley dropped as low as she could get while she searched for her cell phone. She located it and pulled up the sheriff's number.

"He said he'd kill me if I ever said anything." Oaklynn's voice was small and scared, and it nearly cracked Ensley's heart in half.

"Your father said that to you?" Ensley could hardly believe her ears and hardly imagine the hell Oaklynn must have been living in if her father had killed her best friends and she'd had to cover.

"Yes. I shouldn't have come with you. This will make it worse on everyone—"

"We won't let anything happen to you," Ensley promised, reassuring the scared girl.

A few moments of silence passed before more sobs racked the young woman in the backseat who, in that moment, sounded so much like the same little girl.

"Can I see the picture of Cooper again?"

Ensley reached inside her bag as she fumbled with her cell. She held the photo in front of Oaklynn. Levi swerved and she grabbed the seat to balance herself, losing her grip on the picture. With no idea where it had gone and no time to waste, Ensley called the sheriff.

Justice answered on the second ring.

"Shots are being fired at us. We're heading westbound toward town from Stock's Farm and Oaklynn Stock is in the vehicle with us," Ensley said, realizing she'd just thrown a lot of information at the sheriff.

"Okay. I'm on my way. Are you in Levi's vehicle?" Rustling sounds came through the line and the sheriff's breaths quickened. It sounded like she was sprinting toward her vehicle.

"Yes." Adrenaline spiked and Ensley's pulse skyrocketed. She glanced up at Levi and her heart fisted.

"We have company." His gaze was fixed on his rearview for a few seconds and then he refocused on the road ahead. "Both ways."

Ensley scrambled to get a better view. A truck barreled toward them from behind. In front was no better. A truck was turned sideways, blocking the two-lane road. From this distance, all she could see was the driver's side door open, a glint of metal, and a male figure.

"Hold on." Levi slammed on the brakes.

Ensley braced herself with one hand planted on the seat in front of them and the other gripping the headrest behind. The cell went flying onto the floorboard. Karma rebalanced after dropping down on his belly. The fact he was calm said he was used to this and she remembered he could've easily been in similar situations during his time of service.

There was a field to the left and scrub brush with trees to the right, so it wasn't hard to figure out which way to turn. The ride got a whole lot bouncier as Levi swerved, exiting the road.

"Buckle up," was all he said. Ensley quickly complied, helping Oaklynn secure her belt next.

Ensley felt around on the floorboard for the cell. When she couldn't find it, she started calling out everything she could see. "Black truck blocking the road. Mr. Stock's pickup behind us. Uncertain if he's alone."

"Daddy?" Oaklynn cried out and her concern made Ensley wonder if the man was innocent.

"Did your father murder Cooper and Greyson?" Ensley figured she might as well ask now. She had no idea if she'd get the chance again.

"No." The word was final and not the one Ensley expected.

"Who is he covering for then? The mayor?" she pushed.

"My brother," Oaklynn finally said. "It was Ren and Becks. They found out about our plans and showed up that night. Becks got out of hand, stalking us and scaring us to death. We ran and he split us up..."

Oaklynn was sobbing now. Dry heaves ripped through her.

"I didn't know what to do. He was scaring us and then he caught Cooper. Cooper yelled at him and called him a bunch of names. And then Becks just…"

Oaklynn brought her hands up to her face and cried. She had a death grip on Cooper's picture.

"My brother told him he was being a jerk and taking everything too far. They started yelling at each other and then he did it. Becks's hand slipped or something and…there was so much blood. Greyson freaked out and Becks forced my brother to kill him so my brother couldn't rat him out."

"Where were you while this was happening?" Hearing the truth after all this time sent a mix of emotions swirling through Ensley. Her heart hurt. She physically ached. But there was something freeing about knowing what happened.

"I was standing behind a tree, too scared to say or do anything. I should've…" More sobs racked her. It took a minute to continue. "I should've said something but Becks was out of control and wasn't listening to reason. My brother started freaking out, saying Becks would get away with it and he would be the one blamed. So, I ran away."

Ensley knew the rest of the story. Oaklynn got lost in the woods for days before being found. What she'd been through was beyond hell. Though it didn't excuse her from not telling the truth by any means, Ensley found herself understanding the impossible situation that Oaklynn had found herself in, and mourning the innocence that the girl had lost the night her best friends were murdered.

"By the time I was found, I'd tried to block everything out and I did for a long time. Pieces of it came back to me. My brother started acting so different but everyone seemed to write his behavior off as hard times. My father figured out that I was starting to remember. Bits and pieces would come back in nightmares. He said telling anyone would just make it worse. He said they'd kill my brother if he wasn't tortured first. I know he didn't want to do what he did...it's no excuse, but I heard him screaming and crying after he killed Greyson. He was never right in the mind after that night."

More sobs racked her.

"The backpack was so they could find the place again. Becks said they had to find me and make sure I didn't see what had—"

The sound of a bullet splitting the air stopped her mid-sentence.

"Hold tight." Levi swerved so hard that Ensley could've sworn the truck went up on two wheels.

Another bullet cracked as Levi made a beeline for the trees ahead. The woods were close and the truck behind them was gaining ground. Levi spun the wheel right. Panic slammed into Ensley when she realized they were about to be trapped.

Levi muttered the same curses she was thinking as

he skidded toward the tree line and then stopped the truck.

"Karma and I can handle these guys." He reached underneath his seat and produced a handgun. "You two head into the trees and find a place to hide. Take your cell and turn the sound off."

There was no time to argue. Ensley needed to get Oaklynn out of there and as far away from her father as possible. She scrambled to unbuckle her seatbelt and find her phone. Her hands shook from adrenaline and she came up empty on the cell front. There was no time.

"Come on," she urged Oaklynn, who was clinging to the picture of Cooper. The fact she'd been forced to go back to what was supposed to resemble a normal life after witnessing her two best friends being murdered at the hands of her brother and Becks was unthinkable.

Ensley could barely imagine how horrific that must've been for Oaklynn after experiencing unimaginable trauma. Her father's need to sweep the murders under the rug like they'd never happened, along with the mayor's influence to bury the facts, burned Ensley from the inside out. She wanted to be there when the bastard was arrested because those fingerprints would come back and nail them both. Whoever touched the bag, and she imagined that would have been Becks, had given himself away.

Oaklynn stumbled on her way out of the truck.

Ensley grabbed her arm and tugged her into a full run. She hadn't had time to locate her cell, which left them at a disadvantage. It was late afternoon and the sun wasn't due to descend for a few hours, but she could only hope it would only take a few minutes for the sheriff to arrive and offer backup that Levi needed.

The sound of shots being fired sent fear raging through her. The thought of anything happening to Levi or Karma caused her legs to wobble. Her toe caught on scrub brush and she took a couple of forward steps to right herself.

Ensley's thighs burned and her heart hammered her rib cage. Breathing hurt.

"I can't keep going," Oaklynn said through labored breaths. "I have to stop."

Oaklynn broke her hand free and dropped to her knees. She had a death grip on Cooper's photo, which was now bent and crinkled. "I'm sorry." She looked around in horror. "I can't do this. I can't keep going..."

Being in the woods seemed to bring with it a flood of memories. Oaklynn doubled over and gripped her stomach.

Ensley scanned the area to make sure they were alone before walking over and bending down. "I'm here. You'll be okay."

Oaklynn leaned into Ensley, buried her face and quietly sobbed. The floodgates opened and all Ensley could do was hold the trembling young woman. She stroked her hair as Oaklynn seemed to be holding on for dear life.

"I'm so sorry for what you've been through," Ensley soothed. She kept a vigilant watch on the area around her, but it was clear that the biggest threat to Oaklynn had been bottling up her feelings for so long.

They had that in common.

When the sobs slowed, Ensley helped Oaklynn to stand.

"I can't be here." Her body visibly shook. "The woods...it's too much..."

"Stick with me and we'll be okay." It was a promise Ensley had no idea if she could keep.

17

L evi cursed as a Jeep pulled up twenty yards away. Two men hopped out of the passenger side. They were too far away to recognize, and both wore hoodies despite the moderate temperatures.

Another shot fired but it was too far to the left to strike the pickup. The gunfire was close enough to keep him inside his vehicle.

The truck that Mr. Stock had followed him in sat idle, making sure Levi stayed parked. He cursed as he watched the hooded guys disappear into the thicket without any way to warn Ensley of the danger heading her way.

Then again, he had no idea which way she'd gone. Frustration got the best of him and he smacked his flat palm against the steering wheel.

The Jeep retreated and the sound of sirens came

too late. Mr. Stock seemed to know when to stay put. Rather than put up a fight, he stepped out of his vehicle, set the shotgun down on the hood of his truck and then backed away in measured steps, hands in the air.

By the time Sheriff Justice roared up to the scene, Mr. Stock stood twenty feet from his truck. There was an expression on his face...resignation? Reckoning?

Levi stepped out of his truck with Karma at his side to meet the sheriff, who had parked near Mr. Stock.

"Keep your hands in the air where I can see them." Sheriff Justice came full-on officer of the law mode, weapon ready and aimed at her target. "Step over to my vehicle."

Mr. Stock obliged.

As soon as he reached her vehicle, she was behind him, forcing his torso over the front of her vehicle. "Hands behind your back," she commanded in that tone reserved for law enforcement officers.

"She's in the woods and she's in trouble. There are two men in hoodies...I gotta go find them." Before the sheriff could argue, Levi bolted in the direction where Ensley had taken Oaklynn.

All this time the killer had been living in Cattle Cove. Two of them, in fact. Levi didn't know how much the sheriff had heard earlier. He fished his cell out of his pocket and tried to call Ensley.

He'd been too focused on the driver of the truck shooting in their direction to notice if Ensley had located her cell phone. Since she didn't answer, he doubted it. In the rush of getting Oaklynn out of the truck and to safety, there'd been no time.

All he could think was how he needed to find Ensley. He had to get to her and Oaklynn before the other men. Ensley could not die at the hands of men he believed were Becks and Ren, the men who'd killed her brother. It was the only thing that made sense.

Anger heated the blood in his veins.

There was no trail or signs of Ensley and Oaklynn. Shouting at them would only give away his location and theirs if they responded.

Branches slapped at Levi's face as he and Karma raced deeper into the woods. Rain threatened and the sky had darkened in the last few minutes.

Ensley didn't deserve to lose the brother she so clearly loved. She didn't deserve to spend the past decade praying for justice. She sure as hell didn't deserve to be out here, stalked by murderers. Levi knew in his heart those men had every intention of finishing the job they'd started years ago.

Ren was an unknown, but Becks wasn't. He was cold-blooded. There'd been rumors of him being cruel to kids who were younger than him. Oaklynn's brother might have gotten involved with the wrong person at the wrong time, made a horrific mistake and now the whole family was trying to live with it. That was one thing about the criminal mind that Levi had never understood. Did a criminal ever truly think he or she got away with it? Even if justice was delayed or the offender didn't end up in prison, taking a life changed a person. Levi knew firsthand from his time in the military, and those kills were considered righteous. Did a civilian ever really think life could go back to 'normal' after Greyson's and Cooper's murders?

Levi was very aware of the race he was in against the hooded men. He was at a loss since he didn't know this area. Put him on his property and, despite his family owning thousands of acres, he knew every inch, every fence.

There was no use looking back to see if the sheriff had followed. He'd broken through the tree line at a dizzying pace. The only sounds around him now were those of his and Karma's footsteps as they barreled through trees and hopped scrub brush.

Karma had taken the lead. There was no other option in Levi's mind than to find Ensley. Levi followed Karma, the leash had no slack. He seemed to know where he wanted to go, and Levi had no clue.

The thought of not finding her, of not getting to the woman he loved in time. Loved?

Being with Ensley made him see everything he'd been missing in every relationship his entire life. He had no idea what he'd been looking for until he found it in her. He loved his family's ranch and the land was part of his soul. But once he found Ensley, if she'd have him, he wanted to build a life together. A life without her no longer made sense. Make no mistake about it, Ensley was home.

If he had to move, that's exactly what he'd do. He didn't take his responsibilities at home lightly, but that was just logistics. He'd figure out a way to be together if she wanted the same.

Levi came across the same clearing he'd seen a few minutes ago. As much as he trusted Karma with his life, he was almost certain the dog was lost and walking them in circles. He glanced around, certain they'd run past that same hill with that same rock formation at least three times. He cursed under his breath. And then his cell buzzed.

He fished it out of his pocket and scanned the area. He checked the screen and saw that the sheriff was calling. He put the phone to his ear and, as quietly as possible, answered.

"What's your location?" the sheriff's voice came through the line.

"Your guess is as good as mine."

"I heard everything through the cell phone earlier. I heard Oaklynn's statement." The sheriff's voice was low and he could hear her stepping through the trees.

"Where are you?" It was good that she'd heard. That way, Oaklynn wouldn't be put through the trauma of having to repeat herself. The kid had been through enough for one day.

"I'm not sure," she admitted.

"Two guys were dropped off in a Jeep. It's why I took off. The Jeep was white."

"Mrs. Whitfield owns a white Jeep."

"It figures. They're involved up to their eyeballs," he stated.

"The Beckwiths and the Whitfields go way back," Justice said.

Levi paused for a moment.

"I have to find her." He was saying it more for himself than the sheriff's benefit.

"I know. We will." The unspoken words sitting between them were...would they find them in time?

"Call me if you have another question. I need to get off the phone." He needed all his attention on what was going on around him.

"Roger that. Same with you. You see something, you don't go in. You call me first." That was the first time Levi realized the real reason she'd called. She didn't want him running in hot to a potential crime scene and destroying evidence.

And there was no way he was making that promise because he knew right then and there he wouldn't keep it. If he had a chance to jump in and save Ensley or Oaklynn, he wouldn't hesitate. One of the main advantages of being a rancher and not a lawman was that he didn't have to follow protocol.

Granted, he wouldn't purposely destroy evidence. But if there was an injured person, he wouldn't hesitate to get to them. To Ensley. Evidence be damned.

Levi ended the call and tucked his cell into his pocket. Nose to the ground, Karma seemed to be tracking something. People weren't exactly his specialty and he could be leading them in the wrong direction.

Karma stopped at a creek bed. The storm was moving in and it was getting darker by the minute.

ENSLEY PEELED her fingers out of Oaklynn's hand. She had to shake hers to bring the blood back. She rejoined their hands and quietly led Oaklynn down the creek bank. They'd been following it along for a while now.

Without a watch or a cell phone, Ensley had no idea how long they'd been out there or how to find her way out. The weather had turned and the winds kicked up. Her second fear was the two of them being stranded overnight in the woods. As it was, Oaklynn was barely keeping a grip on her emotions.

Levi would be looking for them, if he was okay. He could have been shot...no...she couldn't allow her mind to go there. Her heart fisted thinking anything could have happened to Levi. She couldn't pinpoint the exact moment along the way when she'd fallen for him but she had.

Even though trying to figure out any kind of future with them was complicated, she couldn't imagine her life without him in it. He was the 'thing' missing from every past relationship. He was home.

And now that she'd found him, her worst fear was becoming forever lost in the woods.

Being a teenager in Cattle Cove, Ensley had been taught to find water and follow it downstream to find a town. She'd never been a nature girl, per se. She appreciated the beauty but never had felt the need to spend her days hiking.

She heard the sounds of a twig snap to her right. Was it Mr. Stock? Levi? Oaklynn gripped Ensley's hand even tighter if that was even possible.

Ensley froze and listened, not wanting to give away their location. She motioned Oaklynn to squat down. The sounds of crickets and cicadas and God only knew what else was out there roared.

Wind gusted, whipping through the treetops.

As still as she could be, considering her heart pounded the inside of her rib cage, Ensley listened. It could be an animal.

When it had been quiet for at least a couple of minutes, she nudged Oaklynn to stand.

"I knew we'd find you." The male voice behind her startled them both. Ensley had to reach back into her memory bank to match that voice to a person. It only took a few seconds of searching for her to realize it belonged to Garth Beckwith.

She spun around and tucked Oaklynn behind her. A cold chill raced down Ensley's back at the sight of Becks.

"It's about time." There was something distant and sinister in his voice.

She noticed a second male figure standing behind him.

"Ren?" The shock in Oaklynn's voice sent another icy chill racing down Ensley's spine.

"I'm sorry, sis. You should've left it alone." The anguish in Ren's voice was the exact opposite of the lack of emotion Ensley had heard in Becks's.

"No." The word was spoken in almost a whisper. Oaklynn seemed to know what her brother and Becks intended.

Ensley, out of the side of her mouth so that only Oaklynn could hear her, said, "Run."

Oaklynn shook her head so hard that Ensley didn't have to turn to see her. She sidestepped Ensley's grasp and placed herself squarely in between Becks, her brother, and Ensley.

"Not this time. I'm not running this time. If you're going to kill me, go ahead. The life that I've been living...I might as well have been killed that night too."

"Step aside. I'll deal with you later." Ren's voice was half apology, half anguish.

"I won't do it. Get it over with. You know what you came here to do." There was so much resolve in her voice.

Ensley tried to pull Oaklynn back and failed.

As she gripped the picture of Cooper, she seemed to ready herself for whatever came next.

Facing down the men responsible for Cooper's death, men now who would have only been teenagers then, sent a raging fire ripping through her body.

"If you want to kill her, you're going to have to go through me first." She stepped beside Oaklynn, shoulder to shoulder.

"Perfect." Becks's voice was devoid of emotion. She wondered if he'd ever had any emotion in him.

Ren was the weaker of the two in every sense and it was pretty clear that he didn't want to hurt his sister. He'd probably even led Becks away from his sister all those years ago.

Mistakes were made. Lines were crossed.

The fact Oaklynn had survived without anyone coming after her made so much sense now. Family ties had kept her from coming forward, long after her memories came back from that night. In her way, she was protecting her brother and sacrificing herself in the process.

"You can't go back now, either, can you, Ren?" Ensley taunted. "You didn't want to do it that night. Not like your friend here. But you did and you've been trapped in a prison of your own ever since."

"Don't listen to her. She's trying to confuse you," Becks said to Ren. Her words must be scoring a direct hit, so she continued, "You didn't want to hurt Greyson, did you?"

A dumbfounded look crossed behind Ren's eyes. His mouth fell open.

"Oh, you think I don't know who did what? Did you

not realize that's why I came back?" She'd wanted to make his family suffer in the same way hers had. At least, that's what she felt justice would do. Now? She saw the hell they'd been living in ever since. The mental prison they'd lived in was far worse than any punishment that could be handed out.

Except for Becks. Looking into his eyes was like staring into the eyes of pure evil.

Ensley wrapped her fingers around the sharp stick she'd been holding. She grabbed Oaklynn and pulled her in front, aiming the pointed stick less than an inch from the girl's jugular.

"Go ahead. Do it. You'd save us the trouble." Becks laughed. He seemed ready to call her bluff.

Her money was on Ren. He obviously cared for his sister. Besides, there was no other move and she was basically stalling for time at this point.

"Okay." She made a move, lifting her hand like she was going to jab the pointed stick in Oaklynn's throat.

"Stop. Please. Believe me when I say you can't take it back. I didn't know he was going to die. I wasn't trying to kill him. I know that sounds ridiculous now. But, I never would've done it on purpose. We were just supposed to scare the boys." Ren's voice was shaking and his hold on reality seemed to be slipping. That made him pitiful and also a little bit dangerous. "Please don't hurt my sister. She didn't do anything to deserve this. She still has nightmares."

It was really hard to find a place of sympathy for

Ren after what he'd done. He'd taken a life and then covered it up. But it was also plain to see he was living in his own hell—a worse one than being locked behind metal bars.

He could serve his time, but he couldn't take back his actions or undo his regrets.

"You always were the weak link. My dad said you'd get us caught someday." Becks, on the other hand, seemed to have no problem with what they'd done. He reached behind his shirt and then produced a hand-gun. He aimed it directly at Ren and then fired as Ren grabbed him.

18

The bullet slammed into Ren's shoulder. His arm flew backward as a look of shock stamped his features. Ensley grabbed Oaklynn and wrestled her to the ground to get her out of harm's way.

A wild shot fired as Becks knocked Ren off of him.

Ren was on the ground, shaking and bleeding and yelling. Ensley had to grab Oaklynn's arm to stop her from moving into the line of fire.

Now that the details of that night ten years ago were out in the open, Oaklynn would be able to get the counseling she desperately needed to begin the healing process. But first, Ensley had to get her safely out of the woods.

"The question isn't whether or not I'm going to kill you both. The question is which one am I going to kill first?" Becks sneered. His teeth shone as a look of pure hatred and enjoyment covered his face.

Just as he aimed at Oaklynn and fired a shot, an animal burst through scrub brush. The shot rang out a moment before Karma lurched toward Becks, knocking him over on impact. He flew sideways and another shot fired.

Ensley made a move toward Becks as the gun went flying. Instead, she pivoted toward the weapon. Out of the corner of her eye, she saw Levi.

The weapon was jerked from her grip just as she closed her fingers around the barrel. Karma's jaws clamped down on Becks's elbow and she was certain she heard a bone snap.

Becks screamed a few choice words as he fired the weapon again. She was able to knock his hand just enough to keep the bullet from slamming into her. He rolled and dislodged Karma before kicking the dog.

Karma yelped and a guttural grunt tore from Levi as he dove on top of Becks. The two tumbled over, and Levi came out on top. He reared his fist back and delivered a punch so hard Becks's head snapped to the side and he spit blood.

Ensley realized in that moment that Oaklynn and Ren had been a little too quiet. She immediately jerked her head toward them. Oaklynn sat next to her brother, who'd gone pale. She was stroking his head and an absent look crossed her eyes.

There was so much blood. Ensley scrambled over to the siblings, searching for the source.

Levi had wrangled the weapon from Becks and pressed the barrel against the man's forehead. For a split second, Ensley panicked that Levi might end it all there.

"You're going to spend the rest of your life behind bars. Let's see how tough you are then," Levi bit out.

Relief washed over her.

"My cell's in my pocket, Ensley. The sheriff is out here. Do your best to give her our location while I sit on this bastard."

Ensley retrieved the cell and called the sheriff, talking her through their path. She let Justice know they needed medical personnel. She set the phone down rather than end the call.

"It's over," she said to Oaklynn, who brought her hand around to show Ensley. There was so much blood on it.

Ren was paling, losing a lot of blood. Ensley scanned him and then his sister. "Stay with me. We're going to get you help."

She went to work, tearing a piece off of her shirt to put pressure on Ren's wound.

Within minutes, the scene was crawling with emergency workers. The implication they'd been on the ready sent another cold chill racing down Ensley's back.

As soon as the sheriff had Becks in cuffs, Levi made

a beeline for Ensley and brought her into a tight embrace. A range of emotions filled her. Becks was going to be locked up for a very long time. Justice would finally be served. Tears filled her eyes as she thought about how long she'd waited for this moment and how sweet vindication was after being shunned by the town for her convictions.

The perpetrator's day of reckoning was here. Cooper and Greyson could rest in peace. And maybe Oaklynn could rebuild her life now too.

EMTs were already working on Ren and Oaklynn. Ensley pulled back long enough to make a visual check that neither she nor Levi had been shot. When she was certain they didn't need help, she pushed up to her tiptoes and pressed a kiss to his lips. His mouth moving against hers brought one word to mind, *home.*

Levi pulled back and rested his forehead against hers. "It's over. I don't know what your plans are moving forward but I want to be part of your life. I'm willing to make whatever sacrifice is necessary to be together. I love you, Ensley."

A sweet tear of release leaked out of Ensley's eye and rolled down her cheek. Levi thumbed it away.

"I love you, Levi. I realize now that it was instant from the minute I saw you again. I wasn't sure I could trust it, but I trust you. I love you and I don't want you to make sacrifices for us. You have a lot going on with your family and I want to be by your side as we deal with whatever life brings. Being on the ranch with you feels like home. I've wasted enough of my life never letting anyone get close. But then, I never met anybody who made me want to push past that before until you. Where we live doesn't matter. I just want you and Karma to be my family."

He kissed her, slow and sweet.

"I have every intention of making this permanent. There's no reason to wait on my end." He dropped down on one knee and took her hand in his. "I've waited my whole life for someone like you to come along and I had no idea I was waiting. I thought I was living. I've come to realize everything in my life is so much better with you in it. We've been through a lot in the last couple of days and I can't promise perfection. But I can tell you with all my heart that I want to spend the rest of our lives making memories. Will you do me the honor of becoming my wife?"

"Yes, Levi, I'll marry you."

That was all she needed to say and seemed like all he needed to hear. He stood and brought her into an embrace.

He kissed her with that same passion that had been missing her whole life, until him, until Levi.

When they broke apart, she dropped down to Karma's level.

"Hey, there. What do you think about making the three of us a family?" she asked. He didn't flinch when she reached out to scratch behind his ear.

"Are you ready to get out of here?" Levi asked.

"Yes."

The three of them made their way out of the woods. Mr. Stock was cuffed and in the back of the sheriff's SUVs.

Levi must've had a loose grip on Karma's leash because the dog took off toward the vehicles. Nose to the ground, he ran right to the truck to clear it.

The minute he stopped at the passenger side tire and sniffed, he sat.

Ensley's heart galloped as Levi called Karma back and fished for his cell. The trio back pedaled into the woods, putting as much distance between them and the truck as they could.

The second blast sounded a few seconds after the first. Levi pulled Ensley down and covered her with his heft. In the heat of the moment, he dropped his cell.

It didn't take him long to find it. He immediately called the sheriff, who answered on the first ring.

"Levi?"

"We're okay. There was at least one bomb rigged to my truck and I'm guessing the second blast was your vehicle. There was nothing we could do except get out of there. I thought it would be rigged for someone to open the door."

Levi put the call on speaker, and they heard her radio making a squawking noise.

"Stock," came out on a sharp sigh when she returned to the call. "My deputy just stopped Andy Whitfield on a traffic violation. He was driving his wife's Jeep and acting suspicious. When my deputy asked him to step out of the vehicle, Mr. Whitfield decided to run. He's in custody now. A search of his vehicle found the materials to make bombs hiding in his dashboard."

"What about Mayor Beckwith?" Levi asked.

"The Feds are on his doorstep as we speak. I called in for backup when this whole ordeal started going down. In fact." The line quieted for a moment. "He's in custody right now while another team just picked up the judge."

We did it, Cooper. You can rest now.

Ensley finally exhaled, really exhaled. She finally knew what really happened all those years ago. Justice would be served for Cooper and Greyson. Oaklynn could begin to pick up the pieces of her shattered life, and Ensley had every intention of sticking around to help every step of the way.

Most importantly, she could begin the healing process with the man she loved by her side. She'd found her family, her home.

And she planned to live every moment. Because, she'd learned, life could turn on an instant. It was time she grabbed hold of happiness and held on with both hands.

19

Ryan McGannon looked out onto the land he loved as he leaned against the red brick bunkhouse. His family's property went on as far as the eye could see but his focus was on the backyard right now. He could hardly believe the baseball field where he'd spent most of his childhood was temporarily being converted into a wedding chapel.

Miss Penny beamed as she held onto a laptop so Dad could be there from his hospital bed. Nothing had changed with his condition. He was still in a coma, but the doctors said it was possible he could hear us even though he didn't respond.

Dad would love Ensley. She was a real firecracker and made Levi the happiest Ryan had ever seen his older brother. Good for Levi.

Even at a distance, Ryan could see the silly grin on his brother's face as he stood at the altar about to offer up a vow that meant staying with the same person forever. Thinking about making that kind of commitment made Ryan want to loosen his collar.

Levi managed to include Karma in the ceremony. The ex-bomb sniffer didn't do crowds or people in general. He'd been a working animal. One who'd served his country well. And it was his turn to be taken care of.

Levi and Ensley were more than up for the job. Karma sat in between them, facing their cousin, Reed, who had to stand a good ten feet away. Karma had already been given free rein to inspect the area and Reed, ensuring there were no explosives hiding underneath a fold-up chair.

This event was meant for the couple—a public declaration of their love. There'd be a legal ceremony when Dad was up and around again. Everyone held onto that hope, believed it.

Ryan understood their decision not to wait. He also appreciated their need to include Karma and respect his limitations. Ryan felt the same way about his dog, Rogue. His German shepherd had a hard a time trusting people after being rescued from a bad breeding operation. He'd been locked in a cage until his first birthday when animal control busted the operation.

Now, Rogue needed freedom to roam as much as Ryan did. Even if that meant he had to watch his brother's wedding from a distance. Ryan smirked. He wasn't exactly the social type, so it wasn't particularly a hardship to sit back and let his older brother do his thing.

Parties and socializing weren't high on Ryan's list of favorite activities. He preferred the outdoors, his freedom, and working the ranch.

Folks in town had accused him of being crazy to give up a chance at the majors for ranching life after high school. Not a day went by that he wasn't grateful for the choice he'd made. Being a rancher was in his blood. He loved wide open spaces. He loved the land. He loved Texas. Why would he leave all that for something he enjoyed doing but didn't *need* in his life?

Baseball was fun, but he was born to be a rancher.

He could admit lately that spending all his time with his dog hadn't been all that great on his social life. He'd been distracted by his father's situation. And then there was A.J., who'd pushed to rent out the cabin next to the lake. He'd put it up on one of those internet sites a few months ago and there'd been a steady stream of renters.

His brother had made a good argument against leaving it empty after the family that had lived there moved out. And it was making money hand over fist, not that they needed more zeroes in their bank account.

A.J. wanted to contribute to the family's financial well-being as much as the others. But renting the cabin, having strangers on McGannon land, didn't sit right with Ryan. It was only a matter of time before something would happen despite the fact Ryan kept a close eye on the place.

His internal warning system had been working overtime lately. He could feel trouble moving in like severe weather in spring. And he'd never felt more restless.

To CONTINUE READING Ryan and Alexis's story, click here.

ALSO BY BARB HAN

Cowboys of Cattle Cove

Cowboy Reckoning

Cowboy Cover-up

Cowboy Retribution

Cowboy Judgment

Cowboy Conspiracy

Cowboy Rescue

Cowboy Target

Don't Mess With Texas Cowboys

Texas Cowboy Justice

Texas Cowboy's Honor

Texas Cowboy Daddy

Texas Cowboy's Baby

Texas Cowboy's Bride

Texas Cowboy's Family

Crisis: Cattle Barge

Sudden Setup

Endangered Heiress

Texas Grit

Kidnapped at Christmas

Murder and Mistletoe

Bulletproof Christmas

For more of Barb's books, visit www.BarbHan.com.

ABOUT THE AUTHOR

Barb Han is a USA TODAY and Publisher's Weekly Bestselling Author. Reviewers have called her books "heartfelt" and "exciting."

Barb lives in Texas—her true north—with her adventurous family, a poodle mix and a spunky rescue who is often referred to as a hot mess. She is the proud owner of too many books (if there is such a thing). When not writing, she can be found exploring Manhattan, on a mountain either hiking or skiing depending on the season, or swimming in her own backyard.

Sign up for Barb's newsletter at www.BarbHan.com.

CPSIA information can be obtained
at www.ICGtesting.com
Printed in the USA
LVHW111406090621
689797LV00012B/260